CIRCUS OF THE DEAD

THE NOVELIZATION

By

JOSHUA MILLICAN

Based on the Screenplay by

BILLY HO PON & LEE ANKRUM

ISBN: 978-1-960721-85-3

Cover Artwork by Billy Ho Pon
Cover Layout by Billy Ho Pon and Sean Duregger
Interior design and formatting by Sean Duregger

CONTENTS

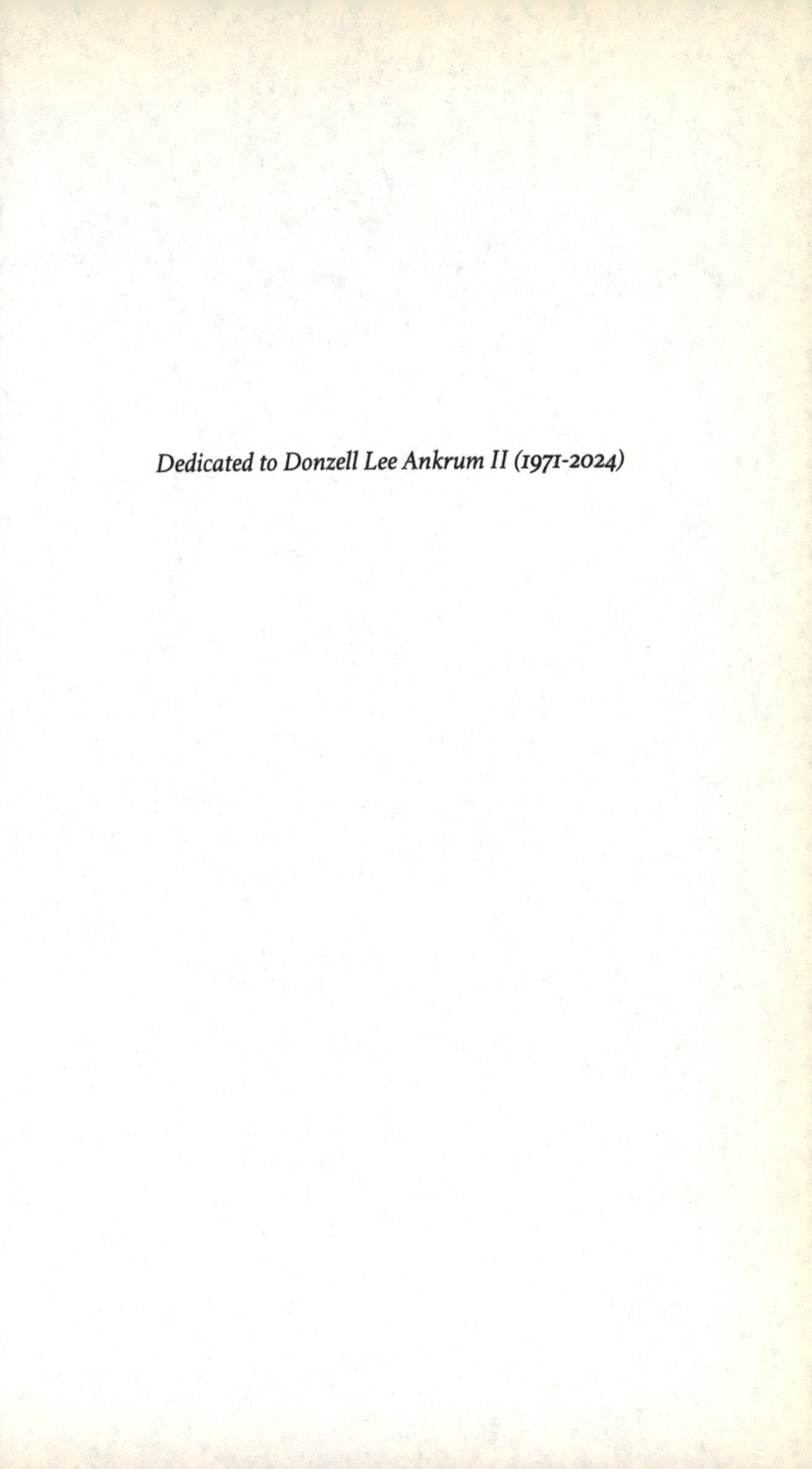

Dedicated to Donzell Lee Ankrum II (1971-2024)

"No smoking, drinking alcohol, or using profane language while in clown. No lewd or indecent behavior. No acts of criminal behavior. Never intentionally cause emotional or physical harm to anyone."

—The Clown Code

"A clown can get away with murder."

— John Wayne Gacy

"Clowns cum confetti!"

–Billy "Bloody Bill" Pon

FOREWORD

BILL OBERST JR.

I do not like Papa Corn.

I certainly do not love him, despite the gnawing knowledge deep in my viscera that he would surely profess to love me. Papa loves everybody. Papa loves you. Papa will always love you. He'll never stop (although you will).

When Papa came to me by way of his cinematic chronicler, Billy Pon, a decade ago, I made a serious mistake. I underestimated him (Papa, not Pon.) In my dismissive way, in my all-knowing naivete, I pegged Papa. Or so I thought.

"Well," I said, "he's a scary clown."

Wrong. And wrong in a trifold way:

1. Papa Corn is not a scary clown, rather,
2. Papa Corn is a scary man, because,
3. Papa Corn is a **man**.

Do you see? Can you comprehend? Do you now begin, with sickening tremulation of heart and gut, to glimpse the naked secret which is the naked horror of He-Who-Drools, of He-With-The-Curly-Forelock? Papa Corn is a man. A man!

And here's the hell of it, the flaming veracity of it: Papa Corn is **every man.**

As Billy Pon whispered in my ear, as I tried to shout from the rooftops, "Papa is what every man would be if there were no restraints."

My God, is that true? Is Papa, in truth, man, mankind, humankind, me, you, us - without restraint? Is what Papa actually does–which is pretty much anything he pleases - what we actually want to do; to eat the whole damned world and smear the screaming juice around our puckered lips, if that's what it takes, so long as IT GETS WHAT IT WANTS?? Let it not be so! Let Papa be a liar! Let it be only a movie!

"Let hell freeze over," I might as well cry. And what's the use? For our Papa has already imagined that particular possibility in a purring free verse I remember speaking for a scene I've never seen: "When hell freezes over," I said, "I will be there wearing a parka made from your family's skin."

No! It's happening. I typed "I" instead of "he" but I swear, dear reader, I swear I meant "he" not me! I meant Papa. I'm not Papa. You're not Papa beneath your own parka-ready skin! We're good people! We're ok. We're ok. We're ok.

Aren't we? AREN'T WE?

Mmmm. Yessss. Let's peek in the glass darkly, shall we? Mmmm, you're wet around the muzzle. Is that drool, or are you just excited to see me? I wonder what's in the cards for you. And me. And you and me. Welcome to the greatest show on earth! Careful where you step.

Papa loves you. Papa will always love you.

Whether you like it or not.

Bill Oberst Jr.

Los Angeles, 2024

https://www.billoberst.com

CIRCUS OF THE DEAD

CHAPTER 1

EL CORAZON (THE HEART)

There's a deserted oil field west of Odessa, Texas. It's smattered with lonesome pump-jacks, dismantled derricks, and rusted pipes as far as the eye can see.

You'll find dozens of what the riggers call "dog houses", those platform offices that also served as sheds, breakrooms, and, when necessary, shelter from the unforgiving elements. Painted blue and bleached by the sun, these derelict boxes are perfect for hiding secrets.

It's a desolate, depressing expanse—but not today. The Big Old Circus rolled in a few days ago, and tonight's the opening night.

You can feel the electricity in the air, can't you?

There's a loud knock at the trailer door.

"Clowns, ten minutes!" a bearded and disheveled man shouts. "Ten minutes, clowns!"

Inside the Clown Trailer, an old phonograph plays a crackling Ragtime tune, "Doo Wacka Doo" by Paul Whiteman & his Orchestra.

A clown sits at his make-up table, illuminated by an antique brass lamp. His workspace is cluttered with jars of lotions, salves, and ointments. Metal cups hold clusters of scissors and brushes; sponges and makeup pads are scattered everywhere. The mirror's stained and cracked.

A mannequin head holds an old-timey police hat with a walrus-sized mustache tied under its nose.

Papa Corn's applying the final touches of his unique, signature clown face. It's a ritual steeped in tradition and reverence that traces back to the days of Phineas Taylor Barnum and James Anthony Bailey. Papa's a professional, and he takes his job very seriously.

He starts with a thick layer of Stein's "Clown White" on the face and neck. He's not happy until every pore is filled, leaving the skin smooth as alabaster.

Next, he uses a fine brush to apply sharp lines that run like needles from where eyebrows should be down through the eyelids. The same brush accentuates crows' feet that convey wisdom, but also menace—like teardrop prison tattoos. He accentuates the chin cleft before applying a mixture of black paint and Vaseline to the lips.

There's another loud knock at the door.

"Five minutes, clowns!"

Under the Big Top, the lady Ringmaster's working the crowd into a frenzy.

"Welcome to the Greatest Show on Earth!"

The crowd hoots and hollers and stamps their feet.

"Who do you want?" she asks.

"We want the clowns!" the audience responds.

"Who do you want?" the lady Ringmaster asks again.

"We want the clowns!"

"Keep it going!" she commands.

"We want the clowns! We want the clowns! We want the clowns..."

The only color on Papa's otherwise monochromatic visage is a tiny blue dot on the tip of the nose. He applies it carefully with his finger, moving in a deliberate counter-clockwise motion. The look complete, Papa sits back to admire his handiwork.

"When we cut out her heart, no pulse could be found," he whispers diabolically. "It was clogged with pure blood that rejected the clown... yes...."

Papa Corn the Clown has made a twin of sorts, a female version of himself. She *used* to be a single mother from Stanton who surprised her kids with an unexpected trip to the circus. Now, she's just a cum dumpster for Papa. After he fucks his fill, he'll pass her along to Noodledome, his most trusted cohort.

Papa spins the chair around so she can see herself in the mirror.

Her eyes may be open, but they won't blink anymore.

"Yes... yes... I know you were going for something 'less Karen,'" Papa makes air quotes around the words "less Karen," "but I though thought this was more *you*! What do you think?"

Papa's sincere, without a hint of mockery. But when she doesn't respond, he answers for her by moving her head up and down and throwing his voice.

"Oh, Papa Corn, you did it! This is wonderful! I'm gonna tell all the gals in the bridge club!"

Papa replies as himself.

"Oh, this old thing? I just did a little here and a little there... your face was the beauty that made my masterpiece complete."

There's another loud knock at the door.

"Clowns! Showtime!"

Papa Corn pulls on his dirty white gloves (with the right pinky cut out) as he and his associates head out the door. He pauses at a wall covered in Mexican Loteria card sheets. Papa pulls a black marker out of his jacket pocket and sniffs it before crossing out "El Corazon—The Heart".

Before exiting the trailer, Papa takes one last look at his latest masterpiece/victim.

Her chest has been ripped open. She's holding her own bloody heart on a dish, covered by a glass dome like an heirloom or a tasty treat, your choice. Her torso and legs are coated in dried blood and semen.

"Happy Trails, until we fuck again," Papa whispers before passionately kissing her on the lips.

He leaves, slamming the trailer door shut behind him.

A quartet of clowns makes their way towards the Big Top. Inside, anticipation is approaching mayhem as gala music builds toward a crescendo. The audience is screaming and stomping their feet in anticipation.

"We want the clowns! We want the clowns..."

"I still can't hear you!" the coy Ringmaster replies.

The crowd brings it up another notch.

"We want the clowns! We want the clowns! We want the clowns..."

"Never let anyone say El Circo Gigante doesn't give the people what they want!"

The applause sound like a freight train loaded with thunder. The energy is orgiastic.

"You asked for it! Now you're gonna get it!"

The curtains part.

"Send in the clowns!"

CHAPTER 2

LA FAMILIA (THE FAMILY)

It's Friday morning in suburban "Waste" Texas and Don Johnson's crawling his exhausted ass out of bed. He worked a ten-hour shift the day before and every day before that for as long as he can remember. Sleep is something he's seriously lacking lately.

His life's become a mundane routine. In all practical ways, he's a zombie; a part time dad and a part-time husband.

He considers collapsing back into bed, muttering.

"Fuck the boss man, fuck the tax man, and fuck both mortgages..."

The snooze alarm goes off for the third time. Don slaps it off, accidentally knocking over a framed picture of his beautiful family. He picks it up off the floor and sighs, remembering those summer vacations at the lake, escaping the West Texas heat.

"I do it for them," he murmurs to himself, collecting the motivation necessary to shamble off to the shower.

Dressed for work in slacks and a short-sleeve button-up shirt, Don finds his wife Tiffany in the kitchen, where she's just finished washing dishes.

"Good morning," she says while handing Don a cup of coffee.

Don gives Tiffany a kiss and a pat on the bottom before turning his attention to the other loves of his life: his daughters.

Dressed in matching private school uniforms, fourteen-year-old Alyssa and ten-year-old Hillary are finishing up their breakfast of bacon and eggs at the kitchen island.

Don beams, walking over to kiss each one on the top of the head.

They barely acknowledge him.

"Hey, Dad," Alyssa manages, without removing her eyes from her iPhone.

Hillary's listening to gangsta rap through her earbuds and singing out loud:

"*There's another girl in the dope man's life. Not quite a bitch, but far from a wife. Just call her Strawberry and everybody know: Strawberry, Strawberry is the neighborhood ho'.*"

Don rolls his eyes, smiles and removes one of Hillary's ear buds.

"You know, Lil' Hill," he joshes, "music has a profound effect on a young, impressionable mind."

"Hi, Daddy," she replies with a smile while reinserting her ear bud.

"Then again, I'm on your side. I always say every family needs at least one hard-core gangsta, ya know? Right?"

"Don, leave her alone," Tiffany interjects. "You used to like rap, too, remember?"

"Oh, I'm all for it!" Don insists. "I loved rap music back in the day. I wanted to live large like a G.O., you know? YOLO, you know what I'm sayin' dawg?"

Tiffany and the girls roll their eyes at Don, who genuinely thought he sounded cool.

"Only problem is, I never prepared for a real future," Don continues. "And look at me now: managing the front desk of a cheap hotel." He sighs, his smile fading. "I wonder if it's too late to sue Run DMC for false advertising?"

"Hey," Tiffany replies, "don't blame Run DMC for the way your life turned out."

"But I guess it could be worse, right?" That's what Don keeps telling himself, every day. Hundreds of times a day.

Tiffany feels Don's mood taking a downward slide and does her best to cheer him up.

"You know, you really haven't done too bad for yourself. Two perfect children and a loving, drop-dead gorgeous wife..."

Don playfully scoffs at her vanity.

"A gorgeous wife, a nice house..."

"Two mortgages, bills up the wazoo..."

"I'm just saying things aren't so bad." Tiffany pulls him close and looks lovingly into his eyes.

"Listen, okay, I know I have plenty to be grateful for," Don tells her. "But sometimes, with this job... I just start to feel suffocated. Buried alive under mountains of stress, and bills, and shit. I remember when we really used to have fun, right? You remember that, don't you?"

"Yeah." Tiffany strokes his face tenderly.

"I mean, I remember when I looked forward to every new day like it was an adventure! But now, it's like every day's just more of the same. Constantly working, spinning my wheels, and losing sleep. Sometimes I don't even feel awake. Does that even make any sense?"

"Yeah, actually, it does," Tiffany tells him. "But I think everyone feels that way at times."

"So, what's the point then?" he asks his wife, not because he's temperamental or contrarian, but because he genuinely wants to know.

"I don't know, Don," she admits, but tries to explain anyway. "Maybe the point is to find joy even in the little things. I'm not gonna lie. I feel the same pressure sometimes. But I find ways to relieve the stress and take my mind off of everything."

"That is true." Don stares intently at his wife. "I know you're right. I am grateful. When I think of you and the rugrats over there, it makes me happy. Really happy. And damn lucky, too. If I didn't have y'all, I'd be lost. I wouldn't be anything. If I didn't have y'all, I just wouldn't want to be alive."

Tiffany's moved to tears. She takes Don's hands and holds them together against her chest.

"Hopefully, you'll never have to worry about that."

Now Don's a little teary-eyed as well.

"Look, just get through your day," Tiffany soothes. "And tonight, we'll go to the circus! All of us, including Lil' Miss Hardcore Gangsta over there."

Don's heart sinks.

"Oh shit, is it Friday already?"

"Don't tell me you forgot!" Tiffany's clearly disappointed.

"I did," Don confesses. "I told Rodriguez I'd work late for him. Shit! I'll have to find someone else to cover for me."

"You better," Tiffany replies. "The girls are so excited about going. They've been talking about it all week long...."

"That sounds great," Don says with a smile, trying with all his might to match his wife's enthusiasm. "But first off, don't lie. Those girls," (he points to daughters), "aren't excited about anything outside those damn phones. I think you're the one who's really excited. And if you're excited, babe, then I couldn't be more thrilled."

Tiffany smiles devilishly.

They embrace.

"And tonight," Tiffany says, "thinking about work will not be allowed."

"No thinking about work until Monday," Don replies. "I promise... Scouts' honor."

"It's gonna be a memorable weekend," Tiffany predicts, and she has no idea how right she is.

"Yeah, it will," Don agrees before grabbing his keys and preparing to face the day. "Okay, it's off to Hell for me."

"Oh, Dad!" Alyssa calls as Don heads towards the door. "Will you please bring me home a venti soy latte?"

"Do you know how much sugar that has in it?"

"Yeah, I know, Dad. But pretty please with... *more* sugar on top?" Alyssa gives him the sad puppy dog eyes.

"Okay. But only because I love you and your sister more than your mom does."

"Thanks, Dad. Love ya." Aylssa goes back to texting.

"Hey," Tiffany protests, "Mom's the one who let you have a cell phone, Alyssa. I'm the one who loves you most!"

"Touche'," Don concedes. "But I don't think either of us wants her dating until she's thirty."

"True," Tiffany agrees. "But we're gonna have hell making that stick."

"We can dream, can't we?"

Tiffany walks Don to the door.

"Of course we can," she tells him. "Of course we can dream."

They embrace again and hold it for a few moments longer

than they do on an average morning. Don wishes he could lose himself in her arms forever. But he can't.

Hell awaits.

CHAPTER 3

CLUB DE DESAYUNO (THE BREAKFAST CLUB)

It's midmorning and Officer T.C. Carter pulls into the parking lot of a greasy spoon off of Business 20 (formerly the old Highway 20).

Pancake Alley #10's been clogging arteries since the 1940s. It doesn't look like much from the outside. The red and white corrugated roof needs to be replaced. The hand-painted sign is fading. The cartoonish mascot, a chef flipping three flapjacks in a single pan, looks depressingly out of date.

As T.C. makes his way inside, he notices a poster for The Big Old Circus taped to the glass door. He pauses briefly and shakes his head.

No, thank you, he says to himself.

Compared to the exterior, the inside of Pancake Alley #10 is damn charming. In fact, it's downright pleasant (if you don't mind the cigarette smoke in the air).

The red walls are freshly painted, the curtains are new,

and the floors and windows are clean. There's a row of comfy booths parallel to the lunch counter; the kitchen's lively with sizzling and chatter.

A chubby apron-clad Hispanic cook wearing a hair-net sets an order on a sill and rings a bell; waitresses in pink serve plates and sling coffee.

"Fool for a Blonde" by Roger Bartlett plays, barely audible over the friendly din of multiple conversations.

The clientele at this hour's mostly geriatric; folks who finished their breakfasts but don't have anything else urgent to do.

A quartet of geezers, all retired drillers, are sitting in a booth, playing dominos while arguing over who's the greatest country western singer of all time.

"I'm telling you boys, for my money I'd say The Possum."

That's Skip Sanders. He's wearing a trucker cap and a flannel shirt. His pockets are filled with scratch off-lottery tickets and a pack of Perro Azul (Blue Dog) cigarettes.

"Yes, sir! George Jones is the Rolls-Royce of Country Music," Troy Dogget, smoking an unfiltered Lucky Strike, agrees before rattling off a couple of his personal favorites: "'He Stop Lovin' Her Today,' 'If Drinkin' Don't Kill Me (Her Memory Will)'..."

"Oh, he's a good one for sure." Lonnie Hopper's got thick glasses and long white hair pulled back into a ponytail. "But I'd have to say, hands down, the best was Conway Twitty. 'Hello Darlin' and 'Touch the Hand' are, pardon my French, goddamn masterpieces. They didn't call him The High Priest of Country Music for nothin'."

"Pussy!"

Gene Jenkins, a decorated veteran, is the most-crotchety member of the crew. He's got a goiter the size of a golf ball growing out of his neck and squinting eyes that never seem to fully open anymore. He scoffs and regards Lonnie with disdain.

Lonnie's taken aback.

"Who you callin' a pussy, Gene?"

"I'm callin' Conway Twitty a pussy!"

Skip chuckles.

"Why the hell are you callin' the great Conway Twitty a pussy?"

"Because it's the goddamn truth. Conway Twitty's a pussy!"

"I sure hope there's a valid reason for your disdain," Skip replies.

"Sure is," Gene says before taking a stroll down Memory Lane... "'Nineteen... seventy-three... Dallas. The old Debonair Club... Me and the future missus were there and that sum bitch tried to put the moves on her!"

The other old men smile. Gene's got a special way of spinning yarns.

"He does his..." (Gene lowers his voice several octaves for his imitation), "'Hello, darling, I'm Conway Twitty'" (Gene returns to his normal voice) "I say, 'Hey fella, she's with me!' So, he says," (in his Conway Twitty voice,) "I didn't mean no harm there, fella. I just wanted to say howdy.'" (Normal voice again.) "So, I said, 'Well, ya said yer howdy, now let us get back to our drinkin!'"

"Then what happened?" Skip asks.

"Well," Gene continues, "he went to play some pool, but the whole time he kept on makin' eyes at Carolyn. And after ten minutes of his winkin' and a wavin', I just walked over and punched him in his goddamn face."

The other geezers are shocked.

"You did not!" Troy challenges.

"The hell I didn't," Gene insists. "And the chicken shit

thing was, he didn't even try to fight back. He jus' laid there and bled all over my boots. *Pussy!*"

The old gentlemen laugh out loud.

"Hey wait!" Troy interjects. "Don't you think we should throw Buck Owens in there somewhere?"

Gene, Skip and Lonnie all look at each other and then back to Troy.

"No!" they reply as one.

When T.C. enters the building, everyone turns to give him a friendly nod or wave. It wasn't always easy being a black man in West Texas, especially a black man with authority. But these were good people, standup members of the community who had always done right by him—for the most part.

"Howdy, T.C.!" Gene says.

A forty-year-old waitress named Flo saunters by.

"Hi, T.C." she says with a smile and a wink.

T.C. smiles back.

"Hey there, Flo."

T.C. heads towards his two associates sitting at the counter near the back: Detective Darwin Roper and City of Odessa Coroner Steve Roscoe.

T.C. meanders over and takes a seat beside them.

"What's up, guys?" he asks.

"Hey there, T.C. How's it going?" Steve, the coroner, is just a few short years away from retirement. He's a portly man who likes to dress in all white. He's great at his job, but he's constantly distracted (most likely on account of ADHD).

"What's up, T.C.?" Detective Roper's in his mid-fifties. He doesn't just wear a cowboy hat; he looks like he was *born* in one. And that hat tells you everything you need to know about his political, religious, and social inclinations (as do his boots).

"It's all good in the 'hood, ya know," T.C. says with a grin.

A friendly waitress named Vera brings T.C. a cup of coffee.

"What cha havin' today, hun?" she asks.

"Oh... the usual's fine, Vera," T.C. replies with a wink.

"That's some burnt shit on toast, comin' right up." She writes up a ticket and puts it up for the cook.

"Any big plans this weekend, guys?" T.C. asks his associates while sipping coffee.

"Well, me and Mama are taking the grandkids out to The Big Old Circus on Saturday night," Steve replies. "Other than that, nothing much, I reckon."

"The circus, huh?" T.C. shakes his head. "No, thank you."

"You not a fan of the circus, T.C.?" Steve responds.

"Something's not right about clowns, you know?" T.C. thinks about it for a moment. "Maybe it's all those white faces."

The guys share a laugh.

"T.C., you know what they always say, right?" Detective Roper grins. "Black is beautiful, tan is grand, but white's still the color of the big Boss Man!"

"The big Boss Man!" Steve repeats before joining Roper in a good chuckle.

"That's what they say, huh?" T.C. takes it all in stride.

"That's what I've heard anyway," Roper says, laughing.

"Is that so, Mister Boss-Man?" T.C. lets them have their digs, allows them to feel superior. It wasn't always easy being a black man in West Texas, putting up with petty indignities like these.

But T.C. oozed self-confidence in every way. He was a local celebrity to boot, as the "hero officer" who pulled little baby Lance Wagner from the well in West Odessa. He was even interviewed by CNN.

"What about you, Roper?" T.C. asks. "Any plans this weekend?"

"Barbecuing for the Cowboy game Sunday," Roper replies. "You boys are welcome to stop by if you want."

"Sounds like a plan!" Steve says. "And I'll have Mama make some of her *world-famous* potato salad. You know she won a blue ribbon at the Permian Basin Fair for that?"

"I think we've heard about that once or twice," Roper replies sarcastically.

"I'll have to check my busy schedule first," T.C. says.

"What's the matter, T.C.? Barbecues don't fit into your busy playboy lifestyle?" Steve chides.

It's ironic that everyone assumes T.C.'s getting strange on the regular, just because he looks like a male model and every single woman in West Texas gets weak in the knees when he walks by. Truth is, he's a perfect gentleman whose mother raised him right. Of course, T.C. does little to dissuade folks of this misconception. *Let them think what they want*, he thinks.

"Well," T.C. replies to Steve, "if I'm honest, your wife's potato salad tastes like shit."

"Well, I'll be!" Steve looks stunned, like a monkey just grabbed his nuts. "I've been eating that stuff for thirty years!"

T.C. and Roper laugh out loud.

CHAPTER 4

EL DIABLITO (THE LITTLE DEVIL)

It's the start of a sizzling hot day and everyone at The Big Old Circus is getting ready for tonight's show.

Horses, tigers, and elephants are being groomed and attended to. Men in coveralls pound stakes with mallets and test cable tension around the perimeter of the Big Top. Candy butchers set up concession stands, preparing to sling sweet and salty treats to the evening's attendees.

Calliope music fills the air, campy and sinister at the same time.

Amidst all the organized chaos, a couple of sweaty "cirkies" (slang for circus workers) are taking a breather, puffing cigarettes and skunk weed.

John Smith's been working the circus circuit for six years come winter. He's already seen it all and knows when to keep his mouth shut.

Juan Martinez joined the crew back in El Paso. A drifter

from Juárez, he claims to be on the run from a borderland cartel. He joined the circus, seeking the protective anonymity of life on the fringes.

When a "worm" (a new cirky) joins the outfit, they're assigned an "Acountabila-Buddy", someone whose job it is to show them the ropes while ultimately being accountable for their fuck-ups. John is Juan's Accountabila-Buddy, and they've been tight for a bit now.

"Hey man, what's a fireball outfit?" Juan asks, puffin' his joint.

John gives him a side-eye.

"Where'd you hear that term?" he asks.

"Back in Hell Paso," Juan tells him. "I heard someone say this was a fireball outfit."

John flicks his cigarette into a pile of horseshit and lights another before explaining.

"A fireball outfit's a circus that brings a bad element to town and ruins it for everybody else. Like, the circus that comes through next is gonna be burned out of town by an angry mob with torches."

"Oh," Juan replies. "So... is this a fireball outfit?"

"Well, shit!" John spits. "Any outfit that's been around as long as we have's gonna have its underbelly. Circus life attracts outsiders, and outsiders attract drugs, prostitution, and gambling. It just comes with the territory."

"Oh," Juan replies.

"You see how bright an' colorful these tents are?" John asks Juan. "You see how everything on the outside sparkles?"

Juan shrugs.

"I suppose so."

"But it's not so pretty in the backyard, right?" The "backyard," is circus lingo for anyplace that's off-limits to the public, places the townies never see. "The trailers look like shit, the equipment looks like shit—hell, even *we* look like shit."

"What's your point?" Juan asks.

"My point is, even things that shine have a dark side. People too."

"Oh," Juan replies. "So… is this a fireball outfit?"

"Jesus Christ, Juan!" John snaps. "Did you not hear a damn thing I just said?" He shakes his head, shrugs his shoulders, and leans on his shovel.

The duo's suddenly distracted when beautiful Tia Colibrí meanders by on the way to her trailer. The Hispanic trapeze artist smiles at them as she passes.

"Did you see that?" Juan asks. "She smiled at me."

"Yeah," John replies with a chuckle. "She smiled at you cause you're standing in shit."

Juan looks down and sees it's true.

"¡Pinche madre!"

John slaps Juan on the back.

"Don't worry about it, amigo. You don't want to get involved with Tia, anyway. She's an iron jaw."

Juan looks confused.

"An iron-jaw. What's that?"

"That's a trapeze artist who holds on by her teeth."

"Oh. Well, what's that got to do with anything?"

"You wanna put your dick in that bear-trap, be my guest!"

Juan thinks about it for a moment and shivers, turning his attention back to his shitty foot. As he wipes his shoe across the dirt, he notices a Loteria card on the ground. He picks it up and flips it over, revealing El Diablito—The Devil.

"Whoa," Juan smiles. "I haven't seen one of these since I was a kid."

"What is it?" John asks "A Tarot Card?"

"No, man, not even close. It's a game for children," Juan

explains. "Me and my grandma used to play this when I was a kid. Basically, it's like Bingo, but from Mexico."

"A game for kids? So, why's there a devil on it?" John asks.

"Portate bien cuatito si note lleva el coloradito. El Diablito." Juan replies.

"Uh... English?"

Juan rolls his eyes.

"It means: 'Behave yourself so that the little red one doesn't carry you away.' Every card has its own character, and every character has its own lines."

"That's kinda interesting, I suppose," John says. "Are they all so spooky?"

"Well, they're all illustrated with Hispanic folk art, but some of them are sillier than others."

"How many of them are there in total?"

"Fifty-two... no, fifty-four, I think," Juan replies. "Just like a normal deck of cards."

"Well, look at that," John says. "You're the one teachin' me something new today! But where do you think it came from?"

"No idea," Juan replies. "I'm just the new guy, remember?"

Their friendly laughter trickles off when Papa Corn casually walks in between them on his way to the Clown Trailer. There's something uncanny and intimidating about the sinewy clown that cools the atmosphere.

Papa Corn pretends to pay them no mind, though he's been eavesdropping on their conversation.

"Whoa," Juan says while reaching into his shirt pocket for another joint. "Who's that guy?"

"That, my amigo, is Papa Corn the Clown."

They think they're talking quietly, but at the mention of his name, Papa Corn turns, grins, and gives the men a bow. His smile's charming and disarming, but also creepy.

In addition to his predominantly white face paint, Papa

wears a white cloth cowl around his head. A clump of oily black hair sticks out above his forehead, styled into an oversized curly-cue.

He's dressed in his signature attire: an old-fashioned tuxedo-suit, out of place and out of time, classy yet worn. Papa wears a wonderful black sport coat with tails adorned with thousands of sequins. Under that: a ruffled bib, a black cummerbund, and a Kentucky Colonel Tie (also known as a southern bow-tie)

Papa's loose-fitting slacks, held in place by black suspenders, look Confederate-gray at a distance, but are actually finely pinstriped. His pant-legs are tucked into a pair of Civil War-era gaiters around his ankles. His black leather shoes are large enough to convey comedy, but still solid enough to kick the living shit out of somebody.

As for accessories: Papa carries a flag-themed satchel; a custom bag, or what folks today might call a "man-purse". His cufflinks and buckles are brass. His gloves are cotton and filthy.

His most striking features, by far, are the ones he was born with—his ice-blue eyes, cold enough to freeze blood.

With a bit of flourish, Papa turns back around and continues walking down Clown Alley towards his trailer.

"What's up with that guy?" Juan asks, his voice barely above a whisper.

"Well," John replies, "most clowns are based on European archetypes that evolved from jesters and harlequins. But Papa Corn's something else, an archetype that's one-hundred percent American: The Hobo. The Vagabond. The Tramp."

"The Tramp?"

"Yes sir. Beholden to no man nor institution, untethered from societal norms, free to go where he pleases."

"So, the show doesn't start for hours," Juan says. "Why's he already in costume?"

"Papa Corn's always in costume. I've never even seen him without makeup. Or, if I have, I don't know it."

Juan's fascinated and wants to know more.

"I wonder who he is under there? What's his story?"

"Amigo, as your Acountabila-Buddy it's my job to inform you that questions like that will lead you straight into some serious trouble. How would you like it if I ask you who you really are, Juan Antonio Felipe Salazar Martinez?"

Papa Corn pauses near the entrance to his trailer. He pays attention to a black goat tied to a banister, regarding the animal with kindness; Papa scratches her forehead around her horns and strokes her beard. He gives John and Juan one last "toodles" wave before disappearing inside.

The door closes with an ominous slam.

The Clown trailer's the size of a shipping container and it's still attached to the beat-up semi that hauls it. It's dingy and dented, with sticky pools of liquid accumulating beneath it. The windows have been deliberately blacked out.

A crackling Ragtime tune emanates from inside.

"What do you think goes on in there?" Juan asks.

"Amigo," John replies, "I guarantee you don't wanna know. C'mon. Let's get back to work."

EL TORO

38
EL APACHE

17
LA VIBORA

26
EL NEGRITO

20
EL MEDICO

45
LA VIRGEN

32
EL MUSICO

39
EL GATO

33
LA ARAÑA

25
EL BORRACHO

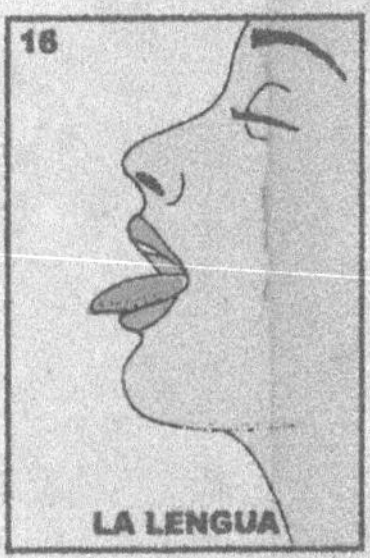
16
LA LENGUA

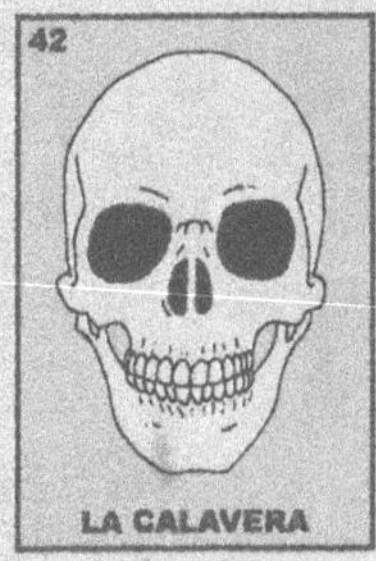
42
LA CALAVERA

28
EL MUÑECO

6
LA SIRENA

1
EL GALLO

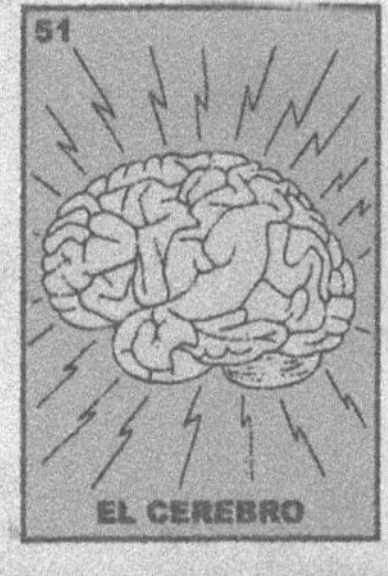
51
EL CEREBRO

41
LA ROSA

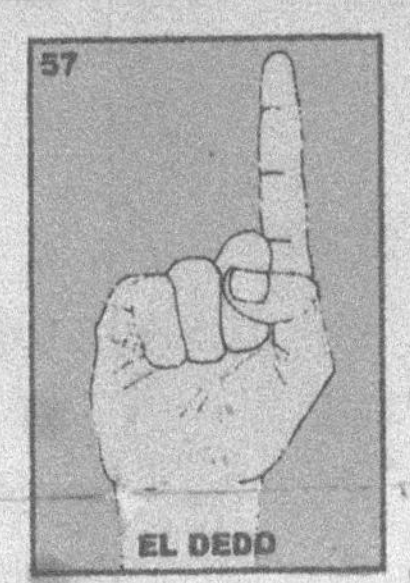
57
EL DEDO

34
EL SOLDADO

35
LA ESTRELLA

60
EL LAGARTIJO

29
LOS NIÑOS

62
LA ENFERMERA

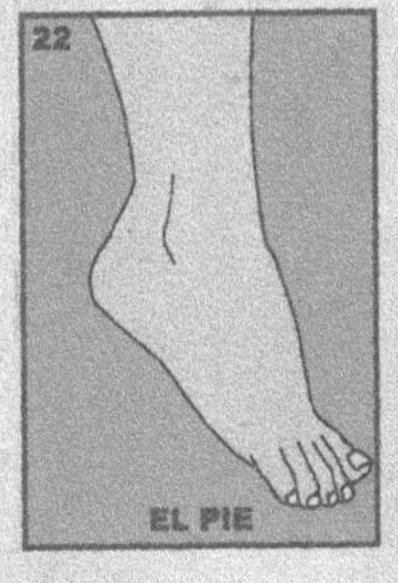
22
EL PIE

8
EL PERRO

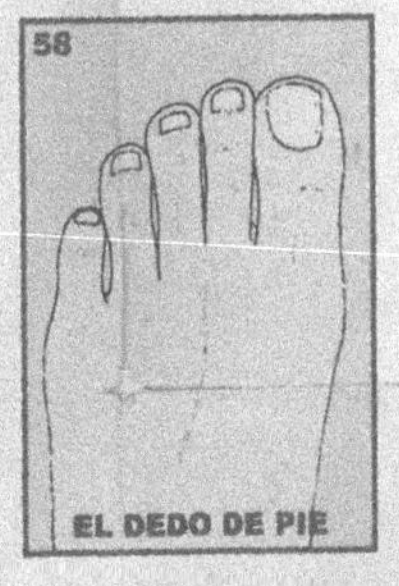
58
EL DEDO DE PIE

56
EL ZOPILOTE

24
EL MARRANO

2
EL DIABLITO

LA RANA

64
EL VAQUERO

52
EL TONTO

EL MOSQUITO

47
LA CORONA

40
EL ALACRAN

50
EL PESCADO

EL LUCHADOR

EL TIGRE

23
LA LUNA

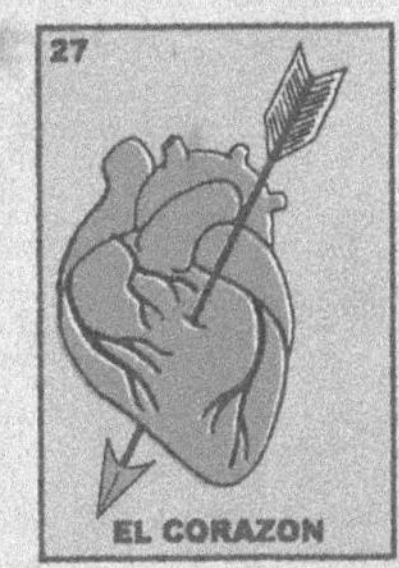

27
EL CORAZON

44
LA MADRE

10
EL OSO

36
LA TORTUGA

48
EL GRINGO

11
EL CHUPACABRA

18
LA MAESTRA

13
EL PAYASO

61
EL ABOGADO

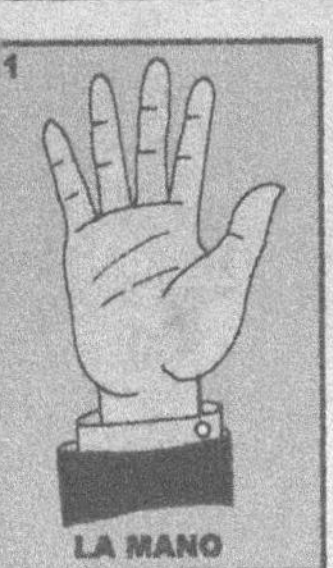
1
LA MANO

49
EL ANGEL

4
EL CATRIN

19
LA MOFETA
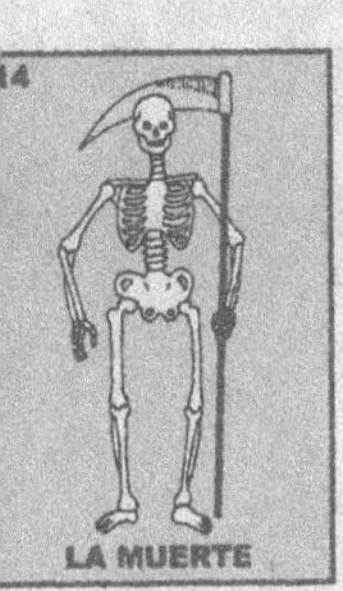
LA MUERTE

46
EL SOL

7
LA VACA

30
LA MOSCA

59
EL MAPACHE

EL CHANGO

3
LA DAMA

63
EL CHINO
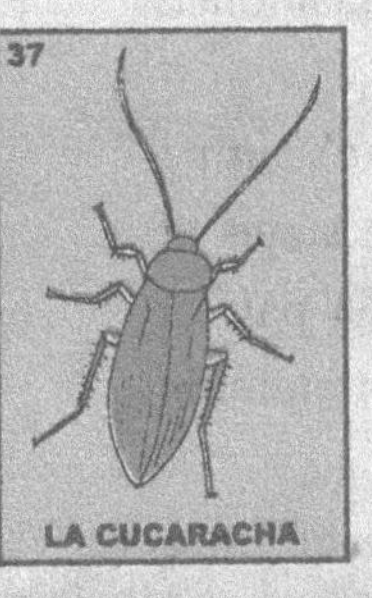
37
LA CUCARACHA

12
EL VALIENTE

43
EL PADRE

EL RATON

CHAPTER 5

EL MANO (THE HAND)

The Clown Trailer is, in fact, a house of horrors.

Even though it's narrow, the space has been sectioned-off and subdivided into a veritable labyrinth teeming with terror. It's packed with classic clown accessories and sadistic implements of torture. The stench is intolerable, but you get used to it after a few days.

Abandon all hope, ye who enter here.

A crackling Ragtime tune plays on an old-fashioned phonograph.

Papa Corn walks past a dirty little blonde girl; she's sitting on a couch with two deceased children in different states of decomposition. She's wearing an Easter Dress and a pair of fuzzy bunny ears. The dried blood and brain matter staining her clothes and hair is not her own.

She's been hanging out in the Clown Trailer ever since Papa and his crew made her an orphan in Little Rock.

She is watching a crappy VHS recording of a Mexican talk show.

"Oh, Gentlemen..." Papa Corn calls out. "Let's get this show on the road."

"You heard the man," a heavy, deadpan voice replies.

Mister Blister Bottoms (aka The Asshole) is Papa Corn's wheelman. Built like a hunchbacked basketball player, devoid of human empathy, and consistently cool under pressure. He used to be a fire-breather, but had too many accidents, leaving him scarred and burned beneath his clothes.

His makeup's a spicy spin on classic clown-face: an exaggerated lower-lip, a red nose (make-up, not foam), and triangle eyes that rise from his eyelids like flames (transitioning from red to orange to yellow). His arching oversized eyebrows crest near the top of his white cloth cowl; his natty hair hangs in limp orange ponytails over each ear, like a droopy dog.

His outfit's sewn from fine satins of black, red, orange, and yellow. His jacket's inferno-themed, as are his bell bottoms with flames rising from the cuffs. He wears a black leather belt with a Zippo lighter in the buckle. On casual days, he peels back to a black t-shirt with white suspenders. Today, he happens to be wearing a t-shirt asking, "May I suggest the Sausage?".

Mister Blister's most iconic feature, however, is the ever-present cigarette dangling from his lips (or clenched in his teeth). He's always got another one ready to go behind his left ear. Smoke's more than just something he creates. It's an element of his personality and a reflection of his toxic soul.

Papa Corn opens a walk-in closet full of half-naked women, all gagged, battered, and filthy. Their hands are bound at the wrists and chained to the ceiling. Though muzzled, they all scream at the sight of him.

"Shh, shh..." he soothes. "Everything's gonna be A-okay!

Ah, who am I kidding? But it's so much easier to swallow a honey-coated lie than a bitter truth."

Papa looks forward to getting to know each of them, in time. But right now, he's looking for someone else. He finds Brandon (the sole survivor of a play date with The Babysitter) cowering in a corner and drags him out by the hair.

Brandon's been with the clowns since The Big Old Circus broke down in Brownsville. He was a swindler and a braggart, a conman and a coward, the epitome of selfishness. But Papa found his commitment to self-preservation impressive, and now he's part of the program.

Papa pushes Brandon over to the hulking Noodledome, who tosses the prisoner over his shoulder like a ragdoll.

Noodledome slams Brandon down into Papa Corn's makeup chair, and straps him down with thick leather belts. He laughs hysterically all the while.

Jumbo the Clown (a mischievous dwarf) runs around on all fours, yipping like a chihuahua and nipping Brandon's ankles.

At four-hundred and fifty pounds and damn near seven feet tall, Noodledome the Clown is the muscle of the bunch—and Papa's number-one confidant. He knows Papa loves him and will always love him. His impish red smile has small rectangles carved out on his bottom lip, looking like buck-teeth when his mouth's shut. His head's bald and covered in just as much clown-white coldcream as his face.

His outfit's cut from the same fine satin cloth as Mr. Blisters', but sewn into a more traditional costume. His oversized red, blue and yellow shirt hangs loosely over his protruding belly. The shirt has puffy white pom-pom buttons and two yellow satin stars on his shoulders. The wide pleated collar (or ruff) around his neck harkens back to the late Fifteenth Century.

Noodledome doesn't speak because he's got the mind of an infant. Instead of talking, he laughs like an amplified hyena. What most people would consider insufferable is music to Papa Corn's ears. Though simple, Noodledome's a skilled craftsman, producing what folks today might call "outsider art".

Jumbo the Clown could pass as Noodledome's twin, were it not for the dwarfism, albinism, and frontonasal dysplasia. He sports upside-down blue triangles under each albino-pink eye; his red cap's topped with a blue pom. His ruff's even puffier than Noodledome's.

Papa and company took Jumbo in after his freak show brothers, Tad and Gunther, were killed in a funhouse "accident" up in rural Iowa. He's fluent in both Spanish and English, but prefers gargling like a goblin and barking like a dog. According to his Tinder profile, he's very fond of vintage hand puppets, hidden weapons, and long walks on the beach.

Strapped to the makeup chair and barely able to move, Brandon screams through his duct tape muzzle, thrashing desperately.

Noodledome attempts to soothe him by brushing his hair.

Papa Corn now stands before him.

"Hi..." he says gently.

Brandon weeps.

Papa produces a Lotería card, La Mano—The Hand, and shows it to the others.

Mister Blister hands a staple gun to Papa, who proceeds to staple the card to Brandon's forehead.

Brandon moans and grunts in pain.

Papa Corn leans down beside him.

"Brandon, did you have a good time with The Babysitter? Yes?" Papa grabs Brandon by the ears and forces him to nod yes. Then he imitates the prisoner in a goofy voice.

"Yes, I did, Papa Corn. Yes, I did."

Brandon whimpers.

Papa Corn stands up and straightens his jacket.

"Papa loves you," he says in a voice that's truly comforting before slapping Brandon's head. "You know what to do, boys."

Noodledome bursts into a fit of deviant laughter as he unstraps Brandon. Once freed, he grabs Brandon by the neck and drags him towards the other side of the room.

Mister Blister pulls down a foldaway dinner table, a sturdy plank covered in blood, piss, and last night's dinner.

Noodledome throws Brandon down on the table and straps him down with some help from Jumbo.

Mister Blister forces Brandon's left arm into a vice-grip attached to the table. He tightens the clamps until he can feel Brandon's ulna and radius beginning to shatter.

"Don't move, asshole," he teases Brandon humorlessly. Mister Blister's as deaf to Brandon's gagged pleas for mercy as Papa Corn is.

"Nice watch, asshole," he says sarcastically.

Mister Blister grabs an electric saws-all from the torture table.

Brandon's eyes grow wide as saucers as Mister Blister activates the loud vibrating blade.

Papa Corn's only feet away, admiring himself in the mirror. He doesn't even watch as the carnage unfolds; rather, he still, in an almost meditative state. Brandon's muffled screams are a symphony, Noodledome's laughter rivals the arias of angels. Papa's at peace.

Mister Blister takes a long drag on his cigarette before closing in on Brandon. Blood sprays on the floor, walls, and ceiling as he cuts through Brandon's wrists below his knock-off Rolex.

Brandon screams.

The saws-all rumbles and whines.

Jumbo scurries around on all fours, yapping like a mad dog.

Noodledome's laughter reaches a new level of intensity.

The little girl on the couch holds her hands over her ears while rocking back and forth, eyes fixed on the television. Though the sounds of suffering are muffled, she sees everything out of the corner of her eye.

The torture continues until the work is done.

Brandon's hand hits the gore-soaked floor; his stump spurts blood. He stops struggling, assuming he's survived the worst of it. But he's wrong.

Mister Blister turns off the saws-all and retrieves a homemade blowtorch from the pantry.

"Smoke 'em if ya got 'em!" Blister clicks a switch, producing a stream of fire that hisses like a rabid anaconda. He uses the oversized flame to light a fresh cigarette before turning his attention back to Brandon.

Brandon's eyes roll back in his head when Noodledome forces his hemorrhaging stump into the fire stream. It sounds and smells like fresh bacon frying up.

Once fully cauterized, Mister Blister extinguishes the flame with the turn of a dial. "Mmm..." He's pleased with his work. "Crispy critter!"

Jumbo crawls out of the woodwork wearing a chihuahua puppet on his right hand. He drags a sack of supplies: duct tape, a rubber Halloween prop, and an assortment of clown clothes.

Brandon regains his frayed senses and finds Jumbo's mutated face mere inches above his own.

"¿Necesitas una mano?" The small man cackles as Mister

Blister and Noodledome attach a floppy rubber hand to Brandon's smoldering stump with duct-tape.

Brandon moans hopelessly.

The clowns rip and cut away at his clothing until he's completely naked (save for the Loteria card stapled to his forehead). They pull him off the operating table and dress him in a baggy prisoner's outfit, complete with a black-and-white striped cap. They bind his wrists and ankles with metal shackles—real ones. Finally, they lock a collar around his neck and attach a leash.

Noodledome shoves Brandon back into the makeup chair where Papa Corn's been patiently awaiting his return.

"Ladies and Gentlemen..." Papa emerges from his contemplative state and shouts enthusiastically. "The operation was a success! Woo!" He pulls the La Mano Loteria card off of Brandon's forehead with a pair of pliers and shows it to him.

Brandon winces. He looks at the Loteria card and then down at his new rubber hand.

"Jumbo," Papa Corn says. "Brandon here is looking kind of scruffy. I say we take a little off the top.,"

Jumbo cackles as he climbs a stepstool, coming pink-eye to eye with Brandon. A blade pops out from the head of his chihuahua puppet.

"Shave and a haircut! Cinco centavos!" Jumbo hacks and slashes Brandon's head, pulling hair out in large bloody clumps. When he's finished, he spins the chair around so Brandon can see himself in the cracked mirror.

He barely recognizes himself. The shock of it all almost gives him a heart attack.

Papa Corn beams at his new recruit.

"You've come a long way on your journey of *self-discovery,*" Papa praises. "What do you have to say for yourself?"

A crying Brandon mumbles from behind the duct tape gag.

"Oh, right." Papa rips the tape off his mouth. "There you go. Please, continue."

"I said you could keep the watch, man," Brandon weeps. "What more do you want from me? I'll do anything..."

Papa embraces Brandon, holding the hostage's head against his chest.

"Papa loves you."

It's all Brandon can take. The clown's kind words are somehow more terrifying than his violent actions. He vomits all over Papa's ruffled shirt and cummerbund.

Everyone laughs at Brandon's dismay.

"We've gotta gusher, boys!" Papa shouts.

Papa Corn quickly swipes Mister Blister's half-smoked cigarette and flicks it into Brandon's gaping mouth. Before he can spit it out, Papa clamps Brandon's lips closed with his fingers.

"Brandon... I like you," Papa says in a cool, even tone before turning dark. "But you talk too fucking much."

The cigarette inside Brandon's mouth sizzles as smoke wafts from his nostrils. He struggles, but Noodledome holds him firmly in place.

Papa Corn reaches for his special pincushion (crafted out of female flesh) and plucks out a rusty needle. He finds a length of dirty twine and threads it. He straddles Brandon in the chair and proceeds to sew his mouth shut.

Brandon's stifled cries are intensified by Noodledome's meddling. The behemoth is making baby noises and pinching Brandon's nose as Papa continues his gruesome procedure.

Papa Corn skillfully pulls the final stitch and ties a knot at the end of the string. To ensure Brandon won't pick his wounds, Papa covers his bloody mouth with a fresh strip of duct tape. He grabs a tube of red lipstick from the table and draws a happy smile across Brandon's muzzle.

Brandon whimpers pathetically, snot streaming from his smashed nose.

"Shh..." Papa coos, staring into Brandon's eyes. "Silence is golden!"

CHAPTER 6

DE FENÓMENOS DE FERIA (FREAK SHOW)

It's nearing dusk at The Big Old Circus.

The evening's first attendees are arriving. They park their cars in a dusty dirt lot before making their way towards the Big Top. The air is alive with festive sounds and delicious fragrances.

There's a small crowd gathering around an outdoor side-stage. It's adorned with posters and banners featuring men and women, both sexy and hideous. The atmosphere feels celebratory but also voyeuristic and taboo.

A carnival barker takes the stage.

Mama Gorda's a heavily made-up drag queen with long dark hair, day-old stubble, and a husky voice. The stout dancer wears a shimmering green ball gown and a crown of peacock feathers. She's flanked by her sidekick, Dickie Smalls (a little person sporting a gorilla suit without a mask).

Mama Gorda addresses the eclectic crowd through a big black bullhorn.

"Step right up, babies! Welcome to Mama Gorda's Freaking Sideshow Menagerie!"

Dickie Smalls hops around the stage, attempting to elicit a round of applause. But the crowd seems skeptical.

"Is that one of them thar trans-sex-tites?" one old fogie asked another.

"Come and be amazed by all the oddities I've collected from around the world," Mama Gorda continues. "Treat your senses to horrors and delights once reserved for royalty! See with your own eyes, Goliath: The World's strongest man!"

A muscle-bound man standing seven feet tall takes the stage. Goliath's wearing an old-timey leopard-print outfit that looks like a bathing suit for ladies. His freshly-oiled bald head and body glisten in the fading sun.

Goliath holds a thousand-pound barbell over his head with ease. Then, he holds it in one arm! He struts and flexes as Mama Gorda engages the crowd.

"He's as strong as a bear—and as big as one, too!" she promises, holding her hands eleven inches apart.

An old fart in a cowboy hat boos and bahs until Mama Gorda singles him out.

"What's the problem, cabrone'? Not your favorite flavor?"

The crowd loosens up a bit and laughs at Mama's dig. The old fart, however, is not amused.

"Bah!" he grumbles.

"Don't worry. We've got someone here for you too, lady-killer. A super-sized morsel. Perhaps you'll partake of... Little Lulu!"

It takes five brawny roadies to help lift Little Lulu up onto the three-foot platform. Her muumuu's sewn out of old tents. She's on a portable breathing machine and barely alive.

Another roadie brings a recliner up for Little Lulu. When she sits down, the entire stage creaks beneath her.

"Pound for pound-cake, she's the sexiest of all my thousand-pound freaks," Mama Gorda regales. "A ton o' fun! And she can be yours for one low price!"

Little Lulu tries with all her might to raise one of her hog-sized arms in a feeble attempt at waving.

"But how do you find her cooter?" an old codger cracks, earning him a few hearty laughs and pats on the back.

Unphased by heckling, Mama Gorda prowls the stage, scanning the faces looking up at her.

"Perhaps your tastes are more exotic. Bestial, even? Then, if you dare, confront your fears and marvel at what science cannot explain and nature has disavowed!"

A couple of roadies bring a sizable cage covered by a tarp up on stage. Growls emanating from within suggest something monstrous.

"It was captured by brave hunters deep in the desolate landscape of Hell's sandbox... You know, Mexico! A creature so vile and dangerous, it's known to have feasted upon women and children."

The crowd grows hushed as Mama Gorda grabs one end of the tarp.

"Ladies and Gentlemen! I give you... La Chupacabra! The Goat-Sucker!"

The crowd gasps as Mama Gorda pulls the tarp away. Then the hecklers start their booing. La Chupacabra, in this case, is a sick Pitbull with mange.

A young girl on the outskirts of the crowd points.

"Look, Dad," she says. "It's a puppy!"

"That's not a puppy, sweetheart," her father replies, pulling her away from the risqué entertainment.

Mama Gorda soldiers on.

"Up next on our..."

"You suck!" a heckler yells.

Mama Gorda doesn't miss a beat. She's a pro.

"Yeah, baby, maybe Mama does." She licks her lips and pushes her tongue into the side of her cheek.

The heckler's face turns bright red.

"But first," Mama Gorda continues, "just for you, Cabrone'... May I present the mysterious "El Muneco"! The Doll Boy!"

A feeling of dread creeps through the audience as Mama Gorda continues her hype.

"Born anatomically incorrect, he—I mean, *it*, is always willing to play with you. Doll Boy is a curiosity to behold! His hammer, an accessory to fear!"

Mama points to a corner of the stage where a watermelon's been set up on a barrel beside a sledgehammer. But where's Doll Boy?

Mama looks over at the stage manager and mouths, "What the fuck?"

"We can't find Doll Boy," he whispers.

Mama Gorda's face goes white.

"What do you mean you can't find Doll Boy?" she asks aloud, loud enough for her question to be picked up by the hot bullhorn.

The crowd begins to murmur.

The stage manager shrugs.

"Doll Boy sends his regards," Mama Gorda announces, snapping back into character. "But we'll have to take a raincheck. Anyway, hammer sold separately, bitches! Meow!"

A few folks in the crowd hoot.

"And finally," Mama Gorda continues, "here's a human anomaly not found in any medical textbook. They've bewildered doctors and surgeons for decades! You'll think you're seeing double! Ladies," she pauses for dramatic effect, "have you ever fantasized about having a ménage à trois?"

Conjoined twins take the stage. Two heads and four arms converge into a single torso, ending in two legs.

"They've only got one member," Mama Gorda explains, "but it's big enough for two!" One of the heads looks happily oblivious.

The other head's eyes are filled with terror; duct-tape prevents him from screaming out.

Mama Gorda finishes her spiel.

"Unable to be separated at birth, for twenty-eight years now, they've shared two brains, two hearts and one paycheck! You'll be seeing double when you see the two-and-only, Pete and Re-Pete!"

Re-Pete starts trying to claw Pete's eyes out.

The crowd's souring on Mama Gorda. They boo and pelt her with trash and bottles.

The freaks scatter.

"All this and so much more awaits you, babies! Only at Mama... Gorda's... Freaking... Sideshow... Menagerie!"

CHAPTER 7

DIVERSIÓN EN EL CIRCO (FUN AT THE CIRCUS)

It's dusk when the Johnson family arrives at The Big Old Circus.

Don parks their sedan in the dirt parking lot and they make their way towards the main fairgrounds. They can hear the sounds of elephants trumpeting, smell the popcorn, and practically taste the greasy hotdogs. Calliope music dances on the breeze.

The girls have changed out of their private school uniforms and are now dressed in their comfortable weekend attire. Hillary's wearing blue shorts and a Green Day t-shirt. Alyssa, now a young woman, wears a red summer dress; her hair, usually braided, flows over her shoulders.

Tiffany looks great too in her blue dress and fancy earrings. She can hardly contain her enthusiasm. Something about circuses really gets her riled up.

"I'm so excited," she says, grabbing Don's arm as they make their way towards the ticket line.

Don's making a genuine effort to be happy, but he's despondent and distracted.

All the happiness and hopefulness Tiffany imbibed him with that morning was gone. It had been beaten out of him by another hectic, demeaning day working the front desk at The Parkway Inn out on Business Loop 20. It didn't matter that today's Friday, and that he doesn't have to be back at work until Monday. Just knowing that the indignities will be there is enough to cast him back into the deepest pits of the doldrums.

"Daddy, are there going to be any monkeys?" Hillary asks.

Don pops back into Dad-Mode.

"Aside from the two of you? Well, that remains to be seen. Doesn't it?"

Hillary playfully slaps her dad for the insult and Don laughs.

"Hey Hillary," Alyssa says. "Maybe one of the clowns will want to be your boyfriend. Then you can get married and have little clown babies!"

"Mo-om!" Hillary complains in two syllables.

"Alyssa Ann, please be nice to your sister! Clown babies? What's gotten into you?"

"It was kinda funny," Don says.

"Don, don't encourage her!"

Alyssa makes a face at Hillary.

"Mo-om, Alyssa is making faces at me!"

"Girls! Please!"

"Listen to your mother, girls," Don says, putting his arm around his wife. "I would hate to have to go back home and miss the circus, you know? Then I could do what Daddy does every night: nothing."

Once inside the fairgrounds, the girls talk amongst themselves, deciding what to do first.

Tiffany notices that Don's drifting into outer space again. She walks over to her husband and waves her hand in his face.

"Don? Don? Are you there?"

"Yeah, I'm here," Don replies, reluctantly returning to Earth.

"You wandered away again," Tiffany says. "I need you to be present for the girls tonight. We're here to have fun. As a family."

"I know. Sorry, hun. It'll be good." Don fakes happiness to the best of his abilities. "Bring on the monkeys!"

Tiffany flashes an awkward smile.

Don grabs his daughters' hands and leads them inside the fairgrounds.

The Big Old Circus doesn't have monkeys. Not after the Great Monkey Massacre last season in Amarillo. What happens when someone (definitely not Mister Blister) gives a dozen monkeys meth? Lots of people get hurt, monkeys get euthanized, and the circus gets sued. But I digress.

The rickety rides and western exhibitions are all mildly entertaining. But the Johnson family isn't there for the sideshows. They came for the main attraction—The Greatest Show on Earth.

The girls skip along ahead of their parents, making their way toward the Big Top tent. Once inside, they find seats near the front row. Tiffany, Alyssa, and Hillary are taking in the spectacle of it all. Don, as you might expect, is living in Mopesville.

Unbeknownst to the Johnson family, or anyone under the Big Top, Papa Corn's scanning the crowd from behind a curtain backstage. His ice-blue eyes zero in on a morose-looking man, selfishly ignoring his beautiful family. He has everything a man could want, the keys to perpetual contentment, and doesn't even know it.

"Perfect," Papa Corn whispers.

Papa Corn's attention falls on Tiffany, who's all but given up on cheering up Don. "Mmm," Papa says as his smile turns predatory; drool descends from the corners of his mouth. "Hello my pretty!"

Tiffany bites the tip of a corndog, inadvertently spilling drops of mustard on her cleavage. She wipes mustard off her right breast with her index finger and licks it off.

Papa Corn sucks his thumb.

For less than a fraction of a second, their eyes connect.

Papa Corn retrieves his Loteria cards from his satchel. He sorts through them until he finds La Sirena—The Temptress. It features a bare-breasted woman leaning over the balcony of a Mexican Villa. She even looks like Tiffany.

Papa Corn spies Alyssa and Hillary eating cotton candy while watching a trapeze artist overhead. He looks through his cards again until he finds Los Ninos—The Kids. It features a couple of youngsters frolicking without a care in the world.

Everything's falling into place and Papa's pleased. He looks back at Don, who seems absolutely forlorn, then flips through his remaining cards. He finds the perfect one.

"And Bingo was his name-o."

CHAPTER 8

ENVIA ADENTRO A LOS PAYASOS (SEND IN THE CLOWNS)

The Ringmaster rides in standing atop a galloping horse, majestic white. Her outfit's traditional but also sexy: top hat, glistening crimson jacket with black lapels, and fishnet stockings. The horse is wearing a cape and mask that matches her rider's.

Someone tosses the Ringmaster a microphone as she rounds the arena.

"Ladies and gentlemen, boys and girls—and anybody in between... Welcome to the all-new Circo Gigante!"

The crowd breaks into enthusiastic applause.

"This is the world's oldest forum for family entertainment! It's rated G! And it's for kids of all ages!"

At the other end of Clown Alley, someone knocks on the trailer door.

"Clowns, you have ten minutes! Ten minutes, clowns!"

Inside the Clown Trailer, Brandon's slumped over in Papa Corn's makeup/torture chair.

Papa Corn, Mister Blister, Noodledome, and Jumbo stand around him, admiring his transformation. He's been their prisoner for a while, but now he actually *looks* like a prisoner (albeit a prisoner with a duct-tape muzzle and a clown mouth painted over it).

Brandon opens his eyes and quickly closes them, shaking his head and crying. He's trying to wish it all away.

The clowns are wearing old-timey police uniforms over their usual outfits: baggy black trench coats, black caps, and oversized novelty badges. Mister Blister, Noodledome and Jumbo all have toy plastic bats filled with hard resin to pack a wallop.

Papa Corn's got a super-charged vintage cattle prod. These were declared inhumane for livestock back in the 1960s and are hard to find. Thank goodness for eBay.

"Tonight is the night, Brandon," Papa says. "Tonight I'll bid you a fond adieu."

Back in the Big Top, gala music builds to a crescendo. There's a drumroll. Spotlights go out, the stage lights come on, and the Ringmaster shouts:

"Let's hear it for the Flying Matas!"

And the crowd goes wild.

"Now," she continues. "Please turn your attention to ring number three. All the way from Argentina... He's daring... He's amazing... He's Boomer Bang-Bang Rodriguez... The Human Cannonball!"

There's another knock at the Clown Trailer's door.

"Five minutes, clowns! Clowns, five minutes!"

Noodledome yanks Brandon to his feet. They line up with Papa Corn, Mister Blister, and Jumbo by the front door.

There's a resounding BOOM as Boomer Rodriguez soars

through the Big Top, landing in a safety net. He hops down, dusts some smoking gunpowder off of his body, and takes a bow.

And the crowd goes wild.

"And now," the Ringmaster shouts, "are you ready to smile? Are you ready to laugh?"

The crowd overwhelmingly responds in the affirmative.

"Let's try that again... Are you ready to smile? Are you ready to laugh?"

The Ringmaster cups a hand to her ear. Everybody cheers at the top of their lungs.

"Then clap your hands and stomp your feet! You're gonna get a funny treat!"

The audience claps and stomps their feet so hard the bleachers shake.

"Who do you want?"

"We want the clowns!"

"I can't hear you!"

"We want the clowns!"

"Keep it goin! Louder!"

"We want the clowns! We want the clowns! We want the clowns..."

"Never let anyone say the Circo Gigante doesn't give the people what they want!" the Ringmaster shouts. "You asked for it and now you're gonna get it! Send in the clowns!"

Calliope music, campy and sinister all at once, fills the arena as Papa Corn and his men roll in on a smoking convertible Model-T.

The Keystone Kops were a fictional squad of incompetent police officers. They appeared in slapstick comedies during the silent film era between 1912 and 1917. Since then, circuses around the world have incorporated the motif into their shows.

"Ladies and gentlemen!" Papa Corn addresses the crowd through a fake bushy mustache that practically hangs down to his chin; his voice is absurdly exaggerated. "We are in search of a lawbreaker tonight... Is he among you?"

When Papa Corn speaks, the other clowns perform hammy pantomimes.

Members of the audience laugh and clap.

"Somewhere among you tonight lurks a guilty party who is surely wearing stripes."

Mister Blister begins to chant and encourages the audience to join in.

"Stripes! Stripes! Stripes..."

A boy in near the back stands up and hollers, "Here he is!" Moments earlier, Brandon had been planted in the bleachers.

Alerted to his location, Mister Blister enters the fray, finds the prisoner, and carries him back into the ring.

Brandon cries out with his eyes, hoping someone will see this isn't part of a show—it's real.

Mister Blister, Noodledome, and Jumbo surround Brandon and lay into him with their weapons.

Brandon curls up into the fetal position. The prisoner takes serious blows to his head, guts, and his groin.

The audience wolfs it up and their sadistic laughter hits Brandon like daggers.

Papa Corn signals his fellow Keystones to stand down before turning back to the audience.

"Has justice truly been served if one had not partaken of the prod?" Papa holds his cattle prod over his head like the mighty Excalibur. With the push of a button, the baton jumps to life; crackling, hissing, emitting blue sparks from its tip.

Even though the audience thinks the act is fake, their bloodlust is real. They're like Romans reveling at Christians being fed to savage lions. They want... no—they *demand* that Papa Corn give Brandon the prod.

"Prod! Prod! Prod..."

Papa stands over Brandon and looks down at his bloody, broken body.

Brandon shakes his head, his eyes begging, *Papa, no!*

Papa Corn shrugs.

"The jury has spoken!" He proceeds to poke the clicking death stick into Brandon's spine.

Brandon seizes and jerks like a fish out of water.

Even Don, the man who couldn't be bothered to share a laugh with his family—even he cracks a smile.

"Ladies and Gentlemen!" Papa Corn shouts. "Thanks to you, justice is alive and well in Odessa, Texas!"

They've brought down the house! The four cop clowns take bows, soaking up the love and adoration.

Papa Corn slips back to Brandon, who's lying motionless on the ground.

"You did good tonight," he whispers before jabbing a metal syringe into Brandon's jugular and burying the plunger.

"Happy trails," Papa whispers.

Brandon's eyes close and... he's completely out.

Mister Blister and Noodledome drag Brandon's limp body into the back of the Model-T. The clowns hold on to the sides of the car as Jumbo drives off stage.

Papa hangs back for one last look at the Johnson Family.

Hillary and Alyssa are looking right at him. Delighted, they wave at him.

Genuinely flattered, Papa Corn removes his Police Captain's hat and smiles. He gives the girls a personal bow before joining his associates behind the curtain.

"Yes, yes..." Papa purrs, wiping drool from his chin.

CHAPTER 9

GANADOR (WINNER)

"Ladies and Gentlemen!" the Ringmaster shouts. "May I have your attention, please!"

It's been an amazing night of thrills, spills, and chills for the folks who came out to experience The Big Old Circus. The show's almost over, but there's one more very special surprise.

"To thank you for coming out tonight," the Ringmaster continues, "Circo Gigante will now give one lucky member of the crowd a very special prize!"

The crowd roars enthusiastically. Everyone except down-in-the-dumps Don.

"Our clowns will draw one lucky number," the Ringmaster explains. "And if that number matches the one on your seat—you win!"

A jaunty tune unfurls as the clowns enter the ring for their final encore. Noodledome's pushing a rickety old cart holding a wire basket ticket-turner.

Papa Corn steps forward and addresses the audience in his kooky clown voice.

"Our prize tonight is a romantic getaway!"

Mister Blister holds a basket filled with exotic oddities: fruit, bubble bath... handcuffs.

Papa Corn smiles as he rotates the squeaky ticket-turner a few times. He reaches in and pulls out a ticket: B-44. There's a drumroll as Papa announces:

"Tonight's lucky winner is..." (long dramatic pause,) "seat number F-32... That's F-32!"

Cymbals crash; hoopla; fanfare.

Hillary's the first one to realize that her father's the "winner."

"That's you, Daddy!" she squeals. "It's you!"

Bewildered Don is slow on the uptake but looks down at the stenciled number on his seat: F-32.

"Oh, great," he sighs.

The audience claps and cheers as Jumbo runs forward and pulls Don from his seat.

Reluctantly, Don allows the wee clown to lead him into the ring. He's placed between Papa Corn and Mister Blister. A hot spotlight zeroes-in from above, nearly blinding him.

The last thing a man wants when he's feeling low is to be the center of attention, forced to put on a show. Don would prefer to be literally anywhere else. But he does his best to play along, sheepishly waving at his happy family.

"Congratulations," Mister Blister growls, handing Don the prize basket and blowing smoke in his face.

Jumbo and Noodledome pat him on the back jovially.

Papa Corn spins Don around and shakes his hand enthusiastically. A novelty flower on his lapel, connected to a hidden tube full of piss, squirts Don in the face. The crowd loves it.

Exasperated, Don wipes off his face.

Papa Corn softly addresses him with a charming smile.

"I'm gonna kill your entire family."

"What did you say?" Don replies. "I didn't catch that with all this noise."

Papa snaps back to kooky clown and says, "I said, congratulations! Congratulations!"

The Ringmaster wraps up the show as the clowns escort Don through the curtain backstage.

"There's just a bit of paperwork," Papa Corn explains.

Don nods and smiles.

"I hope you enjoy your prizes." Papa's voice is different now. Not like it was in the ring. His tone is soothing, almost hypnotic.

"Thanks," Don replies. "I'm sure I will."

Papa Corn extends his right hand for formal introductions.

"Thank you for being such a good sport. What's your name?"

"Don."

"Well, *Donald*, it's a pleasure to meet you. My name is Papa Corn, but my friends call me... Papa Corn." Papa giggles.

Where's he from? Don wonders of the excessively formal Papa Corn. He looks like a Southern Gentleman, but he's got no twang. He sounds more like an Englishman without an accent or a transplanted European aristocrat. Is he some sort of amalgamation? Or a chameleon?

Papa's cadence is deliberate, almost academic, yet still poetic in its iambs. Educated, classy—and more than just a bit condescending.

It's the voice of a Svengali.

"Papa Corn," Don grins nervously. "It is a pleasure."

Papa Corn leans in and whispers, "Donald, you have a very *delicious* family."

Don's taken aback, but maintains his smile, nonetheless.

"Thank you. I think."

Jumbo marches over like a tiny soldier and hands Papa Corn a clipboard.

"Thank you very much, Mister Jumbo," Papa Corn says. "And would you please fetch me Mister Blister," he requests politely.

Jumbo salutes Papa Corn, yaps like a dog, and he's off.

Papa Corn hands the paperwork to Don.

"Here you are, Donald."

"Running a little short on help these days?" Don says about Jumbo with a chuckle. Awkward silence follows.

"I'm sorry?" Papa leans in, like he isn't certain he heard Don correctly.

"Short on help," Don repeats. "You know..." he motions at Jumbo.

"Oh," Papa Corn replies, slightly less jovially. "Oh, you've made a joke at the expense of someone differently-abled. How clever you are! But for your information, Mr. Jumbo suffers from a growth hormone deficiency known as dwarfism."

Don's alarmed and embarrassed.

"However," Papa Corn continues, "the last I checked, his sense of humor was quite intact. I'm sure he'll find your joke hilarious."

"I'm so sorry," flabbergasted Don replies. "I didn't mean to be disrespectful."

Papa Corn's face turns stern—then he breaks into laughter.

"I'm just yanking your chain, Donald. He's a dwarf—and an ugly one at that! Who gives a fuck?"

Don completes the forms and hands the clipboard back to Papa Corn.

"Let's see..." Papa Corn says while flipping through the

papers. "Good. Oh, you forgot your address." He hands the clipboard back to Don.

"Is that really necessary?" he asks.

"Well," Papa Corn replies, "how else will we know where to come over for dinner?"

Don hesitates. *This guy can't be serious*, he thinks.

"Look, we're fine with...

"Don't bust my balls," Papa Corn interrupts. "Government regulations, you know?" His voice is no longer comical *or* soothing. "Just trying to do my job, man."

Papa Corn's ability to turn on a dime makes Don uneasy, but he finds it impossible to say no.

"Yeah, formalities. Not a problem."

Don completes the form and hands back the clipboard.

Papa Corn checks it over and nods.

"Thank you, thank you, thank you," he replies in his "normal" voice. "Adios, Donald. Happy trails. Until we meet again."

"It's been a... pleasure," Don says nervously.

"You and your family enjoy the rest of your evening."

"Well, we've got all this *stuff* to go home to," Don says, referring to the basket full of sexy loot.

"I don't care what little Jumbo says about you, Donald. You're alright in my book!"

The two shake hands one last time before Don walks away to rejoin his family.

Mister Blister approaches Papa Corn.

"You rang?"

Papa Corn strikes a match on the clipboard and lights Blister's cigarette.

"It's that time," Papa informs his wheel man.

"Same as Dallas?" Mister Blister asks.

"Yes," Papa Corn replies, though seemingly distracted by

the match burning down into nothing. "Although this time, let's be a little more... incognito, shall we?" He blows out the match.

Mister Blister grunts in the affirmative before retreating into the shadows, plotting mayhem.

Papa Corns stays, watching Don as he and his family make their way out. He's pleased.

"What are these for?" Hillary asks as she pulls the handcuffs out of the prize basket.

"Never you mind," Tiffany replies. She snatches the handcuffs from Hillary and tosses them back in the basket (where she notices half a jar of Vaseline, a beat-up copy of The Kama Sutra, a classic VHS tape of *Debbie Does Dallas*, Chiclets, chicharrones, and a dirty prescription bottle filled with pills).

"This is... weird."

"Yeah," Don replies to his wife. "Tell me about it!"

CHAPTER 10

LA LENGUA (TONGUE)

The day is done, and The Big Old Circus is packing it in for the night. Animals are being put back in their pens, rides and lights are being shut down, and the last of the attendees are headed back to their vehicles.

Festive music slows, distorts, and stops.

John Glenn Clapp and his four-year-old son John Jr. are headed home. The divorced dad only sees his boy every other weekend and, when he does, he spoils him rotten. It drives his ex-wife Laurie nuts.

John Jr. is rich with souvenirs: a circus hat and t-shirt, buttons and pins, a stuffed monkey (leftover from the Great Monkey Massacre), and two goldfish in a bag. He's got balloons tied to each wrist, one red and one yellow. His face is smeared with ketchup and cotton-candy.

"You have a good time tonight, sport?" John Glenn asks John Jr.

"Uh-huh," his son replies.

"Good," John Glenn replies with a smile. "Now you be sure to tell your mama *all* about it!"

They walk on through the parking lot kicking up dust, making their way towards a pimped-out muscle car. It's a customized '68 Camaro, to be exact; emerald-green with white racing stripes down the hood.

As John Glenn helps John Jr. (and his haul) into the passenger seat, his cell phone rings. He looks at the caller ID and shakes his head.

"Well, well, well," John Glenn says. "Speak of the devil and she shall appear."

He climbs into the driver's seat, starts the car's massive engine, and takes the call.

"Yeah?" John Glenn's already annoyed and ready to fight.

John Jr. can hear his mom screaming into his dad's ear through the phone.

John Glenn revs the engine and blasts the radio before peeling out onto 2nd street.

"Oh, come on, Laurie," he screams back while driving recklessly. "Give me a break. We're leaving the circus now... I know it's late, and I promised he'd be in bed by nine, but for crying out loud—we were at the circus... I have him till Sunday, remember?"

Most kids would be terrified to hear their parents fighting, especially while trapped in a car pushing 90 mph. But young John Jr. is already desensitized to these interactions. His mom and dad fight more now than they did when they were together—and that's really saying something.

"Shit, Laurie! I'm doing the best I can... No, I'm not cussing in front of *your* son because he's *my* son too! Oh, please... are we really gonna get into that now?"

John Glenn is so focused on sparring with his ex he doesn't notice the beat-up white van that's been following them.

"Well, I guess we are!... Okay, okay, okay, I heard you! I hear fine! We're not married anymore, so I really don't care..."

The call drops.

"Hello?" John Glenn looks at his phone and sees he's no longer connected. "Well, that just figures." He puts his cell phone away and looks over at his son.

"So, how'd you like the circus, buddy?"

John Jr. smiles and nods.

John Glenn starts flipping through presets on his radio before he notices something unusual.

"Hey," he says to his son. "Do you smell cigarettes?"

Without warning, Mister Blister emerges from the darkness of the back seat.

Before he knows what's going on, John Glenn feels his head being pulled back and a sharp blade pressing against his jugular. He yelps and swerves before quickly regaining control.

"Shit! What the fuck?"

John Jr. is frozen, petrified with fear. He drops his bag of goldfish.

"Pull over." Mister Blister barks. "I said pull over!"

"Okay, okay," John Glenn nervously replies. "Just don't hurt us."

Whenever Papa Corn announces it's time for another spree, it's Mister Blister's job to procure a reliable mode of transportation. He knows Papa prefers nondescript SUVs, minivans, and four-door sedans, but Blister's love for muscle cars is only rivaled by his love for Perro Azul cigarettes. From the moment he saw this one, he couldn't wait to get behind the wheel.

Scared shitless, John Glenn pulls his Camaro into the

empty parking lot of a burned-out strip mall and comes to a stop.

The white van pulls in right behind him. The doors open and clowns emerge, silhouetted by the headlights.

Papa Corn regards the muscle car, turns to Noodledome, and sighs...

"Mister. Noodledome, would you remind me later to explain to Mister Blister what I mean when I say *incognito*?"

It's funny because Noodledome can't remember his own name—or even speak. Still, the mighty simpleton nods and smiles.

Papa stifles a flare of frustration. No one beats Mister Blister when it comes to perpetrating bedlam, but he has a reckless streak that frays Papa's nerves. He'll deal with his insubordinate lieutenant another time.

Inside the Camaro, Mister Blister commands John Glenn to roll down his window, pushing the blade harder against his neck.

"Daddy?" John Jr. whimpers.

"It'll be alright buddy. But for the love of Jesus... Please don't tell your mama."

Noodledome looms large through the back windshield.

Jumbo climbs onto the hood, gargling like a goblin.

Papa Corn approaches the driver's window, coming face to face with John Glenn.

"You want the car?" John Glenn asks. "Take it. Please. Just don't hurt my son," he begs.

Papa Corn regards him intensely, but says nothing. He turns his attention to his stack of Loteria cards. When he finds *La Lengua—The Tongue*, he smiles

"Doctor Noodledome!" Papa Corn exclaims in his kooky clown voice. "We're gonna need an extraction! Stat!" He hands the card to Noodledome who proceeds to the hood of the car.

Noodledome opens up his rusty *Kung Fu* lunch box filled with unsanitary surgical equipment, a Kewpie doll, and a Moon-pie. He selects a few tools before lumbering over to the opened driver's side window, smiling.

"No, no! Stop please! God...!" John Glenn screams as he begins to struggle.

Mister Blister pushes John Glenn's head out the window and forces him to open his mouth.

Noodledome reaches in with a set of locking pliers and pierces John Glenn's tongue.

John Glenn thrashes and kicks, but it's no use.

Noodledome raises a nasty scalpel in his right hand and, with Mister Blister's assistance, removes John Glenn's tongue with the sick glee of a child pulling wings off a fly.

John Glenn moans and chokes as blood gushes from his mouth and down his throat. He watches in wide-eyed horror as Noodledome leans his head back like a seal and chows down on the freshly severed tongue.

Noodledome waves at John Glenn as he chews. Blood drips from the corners of his smile.

John Glenn gives up and goes limp as Noodledome yanks him from the Camaro by his neck, followed closely by Mister Blister.

John Jr. cries silently in his seat until he notices a chihuahua puppet dancing in his window.

"Hee-hee-hee!" Jumbo says as his puppet dances. "Hee-hee-hee!"

All of a sudden, a stiletto blade pops from the puppet's head. John Jr. is terrified.

Outside, Noodledome slams John Glenn down on the concrete.

The broken man gasps for air. He watches in horror as Jumbo leads his son away by the hand, a bag of goldfish in the other hand. His heart sinks when he sees two balloons disappearing into the van.

Papa Corn, Mister Blister, and Noodledome look down at John Glenn.

"What's wrong, asshole?" Mister Blister asks. "Clown got your tongue?"

"Hmm..." Papa Corn considers what to do next and gets a bright idea. He reaches into his shirt and pulls out a sports whistle. He puts it in his mouth and blows.

Inside the van, a powerfully loud chainsaw revs to life.

Papa smiles.

CHAPTER 11

EL NEGRITO (THE LITTLE BLACK MAN)

It's Monday morning at the Johnson's house, where Mondays always come too soon.

"Oh, I forgot to tell you." Tiffany hands a cup of coffee to her husband. "I'm taking the day off work. They owe me a comp day and I'm cashing it in."

"Must be nice," Don says, genuinely jealous. "What are you gonna do with a whole day off?"

"Probably not much," she replies without looking him in the eyes.

"Hopefully, you'll spend some of that time thinking about your hard-working husband," Don teases.

They hug.

A school van pulls up outside and honks.

"Girls!" Tiffany calls out. "Your ride's here! Let's go!"

The girls quickly grab their matching backpacks and bound out.

Alyssa turns back and shouts, "Don't forget to bring me home another venti soy latte, Daddy!"

"I'm out of here, too," Don says. He grabs his keys and sunglasses and gives his wife a quick kiss. "Love you, babe."

"Love you, too," Tiffany replies.

Tiffany smiles, sipping on her coffee as she watches her family heading out for the day from the front porch. While taking in the scenery, she notices a choice looking muscle car parked across the street. She immediately forgets about it when she receives a text.

She heads back inside, suddenly uneasy about something.

Tiffany goes into her bedroom and begins straightening up. Beneath her robe, she's dressed in the same silky negligée she'd gone to sleep in—not that Don had noticed. They kiss and hug in front of the kids, but Don hadn't touched Tiffany romantically in months.

She's struggling internally. She wants to take a positive step forward but feels paralyzed. She's so caught up in her thoughts, she doesn't realize she's being hunted.

An intruder let himself in the backdoor, made his way through the house and, at this very moment, is standing right behind her.

A dark shadow falls across the freshly made bed, shocking Tiffany out of her contemplations. Heart racing, she spins on a dime, prepared to defend herself.

"Hello, baby!"

"Jesus, T.C.!" Tiffany's still in fight-mode, deciding whether or not to clobber him

"Whoa, whoa!" The police officer puts his hands in the air, his Cheshire Cat smile never faltering.

"What are you doing sneaking up on me like that?" Tiffany hollers. "You scared the hell outta me!" She decides she will hit him, but she pulls her punches.

T.C. stops the attack by pulling her closer.

"I'm sorry," he croons, burying his face into the nook of her neck. His mustache makes Tiffany shiver. "Will you ever forgive me?"

"No," she replies, swooning all the while.

T.C. starts kissing her neck softly because he knows she loves it.

"How about now?"

Tiffany purrs.

"Maybe."

Tiffany slides back into bed.

T.C. hangs his holster on the closet doorknob before joining her.

The lovers fall into one another, giving in to their flaming passions. It's sensual, playful, and genuine.

But before either one can begin to undress, Tiffany stops and sits upright. She's burdened.

T.C. rises beside her and puts an arm around her shoulder.

"What's the matter, baby?" he asks.

"I can't keep doing this. I just feel so bad. I thought it would be easier to let him go, but I just can't."

"Are you talking about Don?"

"Of course I'm talking about Don, T.C. Sometimes I think, well, if he's given up on the world, then the girls and I should move on. But then I see shades of the man I married, and he really is an amazing father."

"I know it's hard," T.C. replies. "But what's the solution? Do you want to end this thing between us?"

Tiffany takes T.C.'s hands and looks into his eyes.

"That won't be easy either," she replies, "because I've really fallen for you."

"And I've really fallen for you, too, baby. What do you want to do?"

"I want you to take me, T.C.!"

They return to their ravenous embrace.

"Take me, T.C.," Tiffany moans. "Take me away from all this sadness."

CHAPTER 12

LA SIRENA (THE TEMPTRESS)

Dorris Pittman's the old lady who lives next door to the Johnson family and, this morning, she's out front tending her flowers. She's proud of her roses and her oleander, her daisies and her nasturtiums. She makes small talk with a plaster lawn jockey she calls Toby.

She has no idea she's being watched.

Mister Blister's sitting behind the wheel of his crew's new Camaro, chain smoking and serving as lookout.

Papa Corn, Noodledome, and Jumbo have already crept around the side of the Johnson's house undetected. But they aren't in the clear just yet.

Mister Blister knows that if this old crone hears anything or gets suspicious, he'll have to kill her. He figures he might kill her anyway, just for kicks.

As Noodledome and Jumbo look for a way inside, Papa Corn rounds the side of the house.

"We need a candy snack," he whispers lyrically. "So here we are again, waiting to be seated at our usual table. This one should yield a pallet pleasing morsel or two..."

Papa finds the master bedroom window and peers past the gossamer curtains. A glorious sight meets his eyes.

Tiffany and T.C. are intertwined like sweaty animals, moaning and writhing in all their glory.

Papa likes it. Drool starts flowing down his chin.

"It's not just the taste of the meal," he whispers seductively, ditching his jacket and suspenders. "It's the presentation of the meal's... stupidity."

Papa Corn presses his penis into the glass and begins gyrating slowly. As the blood starts pumping, he notices a framed needlepoint on the wall inside. It reads: "W.W.J.D."

"Hmm," Papa Corn ponders. "What *would* Jesus do?"

Blasphemy never fails to give Papa Corn a raging hard-on. As Tiffany and T.C. begin building towards their climax, Papa grabs his front-tail and tugs wildly.

"It wants the clown; it wants the clown..." he moans

Tiffany bites her lip, clutches the sheets, and moans in ecstasy.

Papa Corn licks his lips as his pupils dilate and his ass-cheeks tighten. He sprays semen across the window just as T.C. pulls out and releases his load.

"Well," Papa pants. "I don't think Mr. Messiah would do *that*."

Tiffany and T.C. recoil into post-coital bliss. But this beautiful moment is quickly shattered when Mrs. Pittman's lawn jockey comes crashing through the window. The lovers are startled and horrified.

Tiffany screams as Noodledome comes charging down the hallways and into the bedroom, laughing hysterically. She scrambles for her cellphone on the nightstand, but Noodledome slaps it away.

Papa Corn jumps in through the broken window.

T.C. bolts for his holster, but Noodledome lunges and grabs him from behind. The clown effortlessly tosses the cop into the dresser mirror, shattering it to pieces.

T.C. falls to the floor, bloody and dazed. He rolls onto his back and sees Noodledome towering over him. The ogre's holding the lawn boy over his head like a dagger.

"Stop," T.C. shouts groggily. "I'm a police off—"

Noodledome brings the statue down square into T.C.'s face. Not just once, but a whole bunch of times. He doesn't stop until the cop's head's flat and looks like roadkill. Blood drips down from the walls and the ceiling.

"T.C.!" Tiffany screams.

Papa Corn grabs her by the hair and pulls her close. He serenades her with poetry.

"Wolves renting sheep, sodomizing Bo Peep... Mother Goose, can a wing-job you lend? Go and ask Mary, making love quite contrary... Fabled whores know how fairy tales end."

Noodledome laughs and claps.

Tiffany winces as Papa licks her face with a guttural grunt.

"Mmm..." Papa savors. "Tastes like slut!"

Jumbo meanders into the room and notices one of T.C. eyeballs rolled under the bed. He retrieves it and strikes up a quick game of fetch with his chihuahua puppet. The other clowns are amused by his antics.

Panic-stricken, Tiffany sees the intruders are momentarily distracted. She breaks free, attempting a daring escape. On the way out the door, however, she trips on the bloody lawn jockey and tumbles into the hallway, breaking her ankle in the process.

Screaming, sobbing, she crawls and limps desperately towards the egress.

Papa Corn follows, cool and confident with a Groucho Marx kind of walk.

Tiffany thinks she's free when she gets to the front door before Papa. She swings it open and prepares to bolt, but finds passage to freedom blocked.

It's Mister Blister!

"Boo!" He blows a cloud of smoke into Tiffany's frightened face.

Papa Corn grabs Tiffany and spins her around to face him "You've been bad, haven't you?"

Tiffany's frozen in fear.

There's a reason Papa Corn cuts the little finger off of his gloves. He grabs Tiffany by the crotch and inserts his pinky.

Tiffany's face contorts.

Papa Corn raises his pinky to his nostrils and sniffs.

"Just as I suspected!"

Papa drags Tiffany back into the living room and pushes her up against a wall.

Mister Blister closes the front door and follows them.

Noodledome and Jumbo wandered in, too.

"Donald works all day while you fuck all day!" Papa hollers, condemning Tiffany as she trembles in his grip.

"Don?" she whimpers, confused.

"Yes... Donald's like a brother to me," Papa Corn replies. "And sister, you've done that brother wrong!"

Tiffany sobs as savage Papa pulls a large knife out from behind his cummerbund.

Papa doesn't even give her time to beg for mercy. He smiles while stabbing her repeatedly.

Tiffany falls on the carpet, blood gushing from her lips,

unable to move. She releases her last breath as Papa saws through her windpipe.

Papa Corn doesn't stop sawing until her head rolls off her shoulders.

Phase One of their dastardly plan completed, the clowns look at one another and laugh.

"Now, we wait for the children!"

CHAPTER 13

LOS NIÑOS (THE CHILDREN)

It's around quarter-past-four when Alyssa and Hillary arrive home. They hop out of the van, wave goodbye to their friends, and make their way towards the front door.

The sisters step inside, immediately slipping in puddles of blood coagulating in the foyer. They scream in confusion, instantly traumatized—and it's only the beginning of their ordeal.

They're beset upon by a quartet of clowns, the same clowns they'd seen at The Big Old Circus on Friday.

"Surprise!" the clowns yell.

Noodledome honks a horn.

Mister Blister pops come confetti.

Jumbo dances around with his chihuahua puppet.

The girls are terrified beyond imagination.

Alyssa's the first to see the bloody bodies on the sofa. A black man and a white woman. She doesn't recognize them because they're headless but knows in her heart that the woman is her mother.

Now Hillary sees the headless bodies, too. It's more than her ten-year-old brain can comprehend. She holds her hands over her eyes.

"Run!" Alyssa screams.

But it's too late. The front door's been slammed shut behind them. They're trapped and at the mercy of madmen.

Alyssa grabs her cell phone, but Noodledome slaps it out of her hand before she can even press 9. He grabs her right wrist and lifts her up off the ground.

"Don't forget the runt!" Mister Blister orders.

Noodledome grabs a shell-shocked Hillary and lifts her off the floor as well—upside-down by her ankle!

Both sisters do their best to resist, but to no avail.

"Bag 'em up, boys!" Papa Corn commands.

Mister Blister and Jumbo bust out a couple of oversized burlap sacks and a roll of duct tape.

"Keep on fighting and see if I don't beat the shit outta you!" Mister Blister tells the girls before he and Jumbo cover their mouths and bind their limbs.

Jumbo sticks his chihuahua puppet in Hillary's upside-down face.

"No llores niña," he cackles. "We're taking you to see The Babysitter!"

Hillary bawls uncontrollably.

"Tranquila niña! You don't wanna make the clowns mad, do you? If that happens..." Jumbo's voice suddenly becomes unnaturally heavy. "We'll fucking kill you!"

"Toss them in!" Papa Corn tells Noodledome.

Noodledome drops each writhing girl into her respective sack.

Mister Blister and Jumbo secure the tops with zip-ties.

"Easy, peasy, lemon squeezy." Mister Blister remarks.

Jumbo yaps in agreement.

Papa Corn approaches the wriggling sacks. The girls can't see him, but they can feel him. Their blood runs cold.

Papa Corn kneels down toward them and smiles.

"Hello, girls." His voice is soft, controlled, and knowing. "You remember me, don't you? I'm Papa Corn."

Muffled screams are the only responses from the sacks.

"Your daddy asked me to come by and keep an eye on y'all. I'm like your daddy's brother."

The other clowns laugh salaciously.

"In fact, I want you both to call me... Uncle Papa!"

CHAPTER 14

HOGAR DULCE HOGAR (HOME SWEET HOME)

Evening traffic was a mess, so it's well after six when Don finally pulls the Johnson family sedan into the driveway. He exits the car holding Alyssa's latte and proceeds inside the house.

"Girls! I'm home!"

Once inside, it takes a few seconds for Don's eyes to adjust to the darker atmosphere. He drops his cellphone on the table by the door, along with his keys and his sunglasses.

The floor is sticky.

When Don's vision comes into focus, he's not sure what he's looking at—on the couch.

"Huh?"

He wonders if Alyssa and Hillary are getting an early start on Halloween decorations. If so, they seem to have constructed a couple of fake headless corpses. Done a pretty good job too. Tiffany was gonna freak out when she saw the mess, but it shows a lot of ingenuity on the part of his daughter.

But those aren't fake corpses and now, Don knows it too.

He drops Alyssa's latte on the floor where its caffeinated contents mix with the gummy gore.

Frozen in fear and speechless, Don takes in the sight of his dead wife and her lover. He knows it's Tiffany; he recognizes the negligée. It's the one he got her last Valentine's Day, the one she'd come to bed wearing last night.

Headless Tiffany and T.C. have been posed in an obscene, humiliating position.

Unadulterated panic crashes over Don.

"Girls!" he screams, running through his vandalized, blood-spattered house. "Alyssa! Hillary!"

He bursts into his daughters' shared bedroom. Silence. He turns on the lights. Clean. Nothing disheveled or out of place... But there's a lump under Hillary's covers, about the size of a child.

"Oh, God!"

Bracing for the worst, Don shakes his head and starts tearing up. He can't believe all this is happening. The fear on his face is palpable as he slowly walks toward the bed. He peels back the covers and sees—the extra-large teddy bear he'd given Hillary last Christmas.

Don's relief is short-lived. He doesn't know whether to be happy they're not here or even more terrified. He sits on the bed beside the teddy bear and weeps into his hands.

Before he can gather enough sense to call 911, a small and stubby hand in a white glove reaches out from under the bed. It's holding a straight razor.

Don screams as someone, or something, starts slashing his feet and his ankles. He gets up to run, but he's tripped by a chihuahua puppet and tumbles to the floor. Don watches in horror as Jumbo, pink albino eyes blazing, crawls out from under the bed.

"¿Te acuerdas de mí, el cabrón? Do you remember me, bastard?"

Don scrambles to his feet and dashes back into the hallway, but he doesn't get far.

Noodledome's been waiting and laughs gleefully when the dismayed cuckold runs straight into him. Don looks up at Noodledome and trembles, unaware that Papa Corn is sneaking up behind him.

Papa Corn knocks Don unconscious with one swift swing of his Employee of the Month trophy. Anything could have done the job, but Papa appreciates small details and irony.

Don's drops like a sack of cabbages, landing with a thud.

Papa Corn kneels down beside Don, pulls out a metal syringe from his man-purse, and sticks the needle into Don's neck.

"Sweet dreams, Donald... Sweet dreams."

Papa Corn stands and dusts off his jacket.

"Now, let's make like a tree and get the fuck outta here," he says. "Oh, Mister Noodledome. Don't forget to grab the head."

CHAPTER 15

NOTICIAS DE ÚLTIMA HORA (BREAKING NEWS)

The News at 10's going to get huge ratings tonight. It always happens when something big happens—and this is big. All the local outlets are competing to be the first to break the story. Channel 7's on right now.

Senior Anchor Angela Maverick sits behind a large desk looking serious and flushed. A graphic insert beside her head features yellow police tape and a chalk outline; it reads: "MURDER IN TEXAS!"

"BREAKING NEWS!" flashes near the bottom of the screen, where a ticker repeats the most gruesome details for the hearing impaired.

"We start with breaking news out of Odessa," Angela begins. "Two people have been found dead. Victims of an apparent kidnapping gone awry. Let's go live to News 7 reporter Linda Ito."

Linda appears on a split screen, standing outside the Johnson family home.

"News 7 was first on the scene of what police are calling a gruesome discovery. Investigators are tight-lipped but neighbors say this is the home of Donald and Tiffany Johnson. The couple has two children: fourteen-year-old Alyssa and ten-year-old Hillary, both students at Saint Ignatius Academy."

In the background, a police officer rushes outside and pukes on the lawn.

"Back to you in the studio, Angela."

"Turn that shit off!" Detective Roper orders while surveying the scene in the Johnson's living room. "And tell Office Deacon to pull himself together. No one better puke on any evidence!"

"Yes, sir." Officer Goodson finds the remote and turns off the TV.

In thirty years on the force, Roper's never seen anything like this. Not even close.

Steve, the coroner, arrives. He looks at the couch and stops in his tracks. He's never seen anything like this before. Not even close.

"What in God's name..."

"Steve." Roper solemnly approaches him. "It's T.C."

Steve's having an emotional reaction but tries to remain professional. He pulls on rubber gloves.

"Anybody call his momma yet?" he asks.

"No, not yet," Roper replies. "Figured I better do it myself. It's gonna break her heart."

Steve wipes the sweat from his forehead with his sleeve.

"Jesus, what the hell was he doing here?"

"You remember him talking about that new lady he's sweet on?" Roper points to Tiffany. "He never mentioned she was already spoken for."

Officer Goodson butts in.

"Sir. We found T.C.'s holster in the master bedroom, but we didn't find his gun."

"Keep me posted."

"You thinking Don Johnson came home, found 'em together, and went ape-shit?" Steve asks.

"That's usually how it goes."

Steve looks closely at T.C.'s body as tears run down his face.

"Well, I'll be..." He notices a framed family portrait hanging on the wall behind the blood-soaked sofa. "Any sign of those kids?"

"Not yet," Roper replies.

"Sir." Officer Goodson approaches Roper with Tiffany's cellphone. "We found it in the kitchen."

Roper snaps on a fresh pair of rubber gloves before taking the sparkly pink phone from Officer Goodson.

"Thank you." Roper begins scrolling through Tiffany's contacts.

"What are you looking for?" Steve asks.

"For starters, I thought we should give her husband a call. See if maybe he wants to do this the easy way." Roper finds Don's name and presses CALL.

Everyone freezes when a vibrating ringtone emanates from the couch.

"What sick shit is this?" Roper asks as he slowly zeroes in on the source of the sound. He's nearly overwhelmed when he discovers Don's cellphone viciously stuffed into Tiffany's exposed esophagus. Her face from happier (healthier) times shines on the vibrating phone screen.

Noodledome put it there on his way out earlier.

"Now what do you think about that?" Steve asks, equally confounded.

"What do I think?" Roper replies. "I think we'll be doing this one the hard way."

CHAPTER 16

MALA PESADILLA (BAD NIGHTMARE)

Don Johnson regains consciousness, finding himself in Hell. That's what it looks like. That's what it feels like. The darkness is oppressive, and the stench is assaultive.

Don's firmly tied to a dented metal chair. Angry voices are screaming at each other on a nearby TV set; some kind of Mexican talk show.

"Los payasos comieron mi esposa!"

"My head!" he groans.

Things only get worse as Don's eyes begin to focus.

Still drugged and discombobulated, Don sees a hulk bumbling towards him. For a moment, he thinks it's a gorilla, but it's not. It's Noodledome!

The ominous colossus takes off his hemorrhoid-stained skivvies and shoves them into Don's mouth; he secures them with a length of rusty bailing wire. Don struggles and groans, but he's helpless against the whims of the behemoth clown.

When Noodledome turns and walks away, Don finally gazes around. He's stunned by the revulsions that surround him.

The floor's littered, stacked, with mutilated/disconnected body parts, all female. Heads and torsos, limbs, and genitals, breasts, and butt cheeks—all in various stages of decomposition.

Don moans through his moist, shitty gag and strains to extricate himself from the chair. It's no use. He tries to calm himself down by closing his eyes and taking a few deep breaths. *Maybe this is all just a terrible nightmare*, he hopes.

But when he opens his eyes again, nothing's changed. He spots Noodledome working at a cluttered workbench in the corner. He's doing arts and crafts by candlelight. Just when Don thinks things couldn't possibly get more insane, they do.

The little girl in the bloody Easter dress makes her way towards Don. She's replaced her bunny ears with a witch's mask, a crone with a hooknose and warts on her chin. Don's sweat freezes as she stands in front of him.

"It's okay, mister," the young hag tells him. "We were all scared once. But Mr. Noodledome just wants to play." She points to a gang of human meat-puppets lined up against an adjacent wall. "Mr. Noodledome wants to play with all of us."

Don's brain struggles to maintain its center.

"We're all his playtime puppets." Her giggles are subzero.

Don shakes his head, as though he can make the situation disappear by denying it. But he can't.

"Just ask, and they'll all tell you how much he truly loves us."

The little girl pulls off her mask, and somehow, her real face is more terrifying. Dirty and bruised, pale and malnourished. Her eyes are vacant, dead.

She puts on a vintage devil mask and speaks again—in Papa Corn's voice.

"We're your fucking family now, Donald!" she cackles.

Don screams through his gag as the little girl approaches the female meat-puppets against the wall.

Talking dolls use a tiny disc to funnel sound through a small amplifier, just like a record player. Noodledome doesn't know what two plus two equals, but he's a master of this niche, forgotten artform. Truly DaVincian in his aspirations.

The little girl stands beside the first of Noodledome's corpse dolls and pulls a string connected to her back.

She speaks! Her voice is reminiscent of Betty Boop but crackly and garbled.

"He calls me Polly Crop-Top. He thinks my flavor's top-notch!"

The little girl moves down the line, pulling a string and activating the next shredded plaything.

"I'm mixed and matched. I'm his dirty Crumb Snatch!"

Don can only watch as the little girl continues down the line.

"My name's Wettie Winnie. Change me when I go pee-pee." On cue, a stream of putrid discharge squirts from between her legs, creating a puddle.

Don wants to look away, but he can't.

The little girl moves down the line and pulls another string.

"He took me from my *Davey and Goliath* sheets. He named me Cathy-lick!" This one's got the gift of gab. "Our Maker commands us to kneel to receive his special communion. There, he connects steel cables to our sacred jaws. Threads them nicely through our sinners' tongues and puts more than words inside our mouths. Our divine grounds are now reserved for our Maker, so that He alone pulls our cables, forcing us to pray for hours!"

Next in the gruesome processional:

"We're his jigsaw puzzle puppets. He named me Mary Annette. Yesterday my eyes fell out playing Dick Knack Patty Whack, Give a Clown a Bone!"

The Swan's a ballerina. She spins on a pole, impaled through her anus and out through the top of her skull. Her eye-sockets are empty.

"I offered my eyes to Mary Annette so our Maker can make her whole again!"

"And with a lot of goo glue cum-cock-tion he stuck my eyes back in," Mary Annette responds. "Hooray!"

Don's beyond freaked out. His eyes twitch back and forth as his mind spins in somersaults. There are more of them, Noodledome's atrocities. Suddenly, their voices seem to overlap and intensify into a monsoon of doom, building towards a cacophonous crescendo.

"I'm Crybaby! He pulled my string so hard it ripped my smile clean off my face!"

"My name is Speak 'n' Scream Sally. Speak 'n' Scream Sally says: please, please, please!" Her screams are deafening. "Please, please, please!"

"I'm Little Debbie Cakes and I'm his favorite chew toy! Someone's got a sweet tooth, naughty-naughty Noodle Boy!

Don closes his eyes and lowers his head. Suddenly, everything goes silent—until he hears a familiar voice:

"Don?"

"Tiffany?" Don opens his eyes. It is her!

Noodledome's at his table crafting his latest masterpiece. It's Tiffany's head! He's cutting her mouth off of her face.

Don sobs, feeling destroyed

It's not real, it's not real, he keeps telling himself.

Tiffany's eyes open. She looks directly at her husband. She speaks!

"This is real, baby. It's all real."

Don closes his eyes and bows his head.

CHAPTER 17

AMAR VERDADERO (TRUE LOVE)

There's a loud knock at the trailer door.

"Five minutes, Pepe the Mime! Pepe the Mime, five minutes!"

The voice rouses Don from his fever-dreams. Once again, he's crushed to discover that the events of the past few hours haven't just been a terrible dream. Tiffany's words re-echo in his ears.

"It's all real, baby."

From within the dark catacombs of the Clown Trailer, a shrill athletic whistle blows.

Pepe, the Chainsaw Juggling Mime, emerges from the gray fog. Tall and lanky, he seems to slide along the walls.

He sports a very old, leather football helmet on his head. He wears a black and white striped shirt tucked into baggy black pants, secured with suspenders *and* a belt equipped with the tools of his trade (accelerants and juggling pins). His face is painted white with black highlights around his eyes.

Don gasps when he notices that Pepe's entire lower jaw is missing, perhaps ripped off in an accident (or, more likely, removed by Papa Corn). He reminds Don of that "Dr. Tongue" zombie from *Day of the Dead.* Can this shit get more outlandish?

Pepe's a prisoner turned protégé, like Brandon. He recently graduated from Papa's program. Now, he's part of the show.

Pepe stops at Noodledome's workbench where he locates his crude, prosthetic jaw with interlocking metal "teeth." He proceeds to strap it on over his mangled mouth, attaching it to buckles sewn into his leather helmet. Now, he reminds Don of that Trap-Jaw character from *He-Man and the Masters of the Universe.* It's crazy, these random connections Don's mind is making in order to distract him from reality.

Then, as silently as he appeared, Pepe slides back into the ominous unknown of the Clown Trailer—to retrieve his chainsaw!

Noodledome emerges. He carries Don, chair, and all, into Papa Corn's domain.

Simultaneously, Mister Blister opens a storage closet to retrieve a frightened Brandon, still filthy and broken from his weekend performances.

"Rise and shine, dickhead," Mister Blister says while blowing a cloud of smoke into Brandon's face. He slams the one-handed bandit down into Papa Corn's makeup chair and straps him in.

"Have a seat, asshole."

Don and Brandon regard one another. Each wonders if the other's a murderer or a potential ally. When it's obvious that they're in the same predicament (completely fucked) they both look down at the floor, overcome with fear and shame.

Papa Corn enters the room and sits down in his recliner across from the hostages.

"Oh, I see you two have already met." Papa's pleased. "Well, let me formally introduce you to one another. Donald, this once motor-mouthed asshole you see before you is Brandon. Brandon's come a long, long way on his journey of... *self-discovery.*" Papa makes air-quotes when he says "self-discovery."

Mister Blister and Noodledome pat Brandon on the shoulders.

"In fact," Papa continues. "Brandon not only played with The Babysitter, he lived to tell the tale. Didn't ya? Did ya?"

He reaches over, grabs Brandon by the head, and forces him to nod in agreement.

"Why, yes. Yes, you did," Papa replies on Brandon's behalf.

Brandon shakes his head free from Papa Corn's grip.

"Now, Brandon," Papa points to Don. "This good excuse for birth control you see before you is Donald. Now Donald has everything any man could ever want. In fact, he has the perfect life. He has a nice house, he has two beautiful daughters, he has—oops," Papa corrects himself. "He *had* a very beautiful wife..."

Don's rage inflamed, he grunts and strains against his bindings. But it's no use. He's stuck.

"Donald, now calm down," Papa suggests. "And trust me when I say your wife did have it coming. She was definitely dabbling in the chocolate."

Don's angry eyes burn into the clown. *No, not Tiffany*, he tells himself, still unable to relinquish the illusion that his wife was faithful.

But Papa Corn knows everything.

"No? I was there. I saw it with my own two eyes. I mean, how could you have not known?" Papa leans closer towards

Don. "You must have noticed that her love tunnel had recently expanded from two lanes to six? If I were a betting man, and I am... I'd say she's been bumping uglies with young Denzel Washington for quite some time."

Don closes his eyes and shakes his head. He can't stand hearing Papa's vile words about the love of his life. But it doesn't stop there.

"What's wrong, Donald? Can't believe your wonderful wife was capable of breaking her sacred vow of holy matrimony?" He slaps Don across his face. "Come on, Donald! Don't be so stupid and naïve. In marriage, you're either the fucker or the fuck-ee..."

Don thrashes in his chair.

"And we know which one you were!"

The mental abuse goes beyond the bounds of psychological torture, but Papa Corn's just getting warmed up.

He rises from his chair to visit Noodledome's workbench. He returns with Tiffany's head in his hands.

Don's heart breaks anew. His psyche bends further.

"But why listen to me? I'm just a clown. Why not ask her yourself?"

It appears that Noodledome's added some truly creative innovations.

Over Tiffany's mouth, he's sewn the entire vulva and vagina of an Asian woman who had dark pubic hair. The pubic mound covers Tiffany's nose like a fighter pilot's oxygen mask.

"What's wrong, Donald?" Papa Corn asks on behalf of Tiffany, using a feminized voice. "Don't you love me anymore?"

Don would push knitting needles into his ears if he could.

"But I still love you," Papa continues in his Tiffany voice, pausing to make kissing sounds. "I just love you so much!"

Don tries to look away, but Papa forces him to "kiss" Tiffany on her new lips.

"Donald, I'm guessing you lost that loving feeling," he taunts while standing up. "Too bad I haven't."

There's no pretty way to say what happens next. It can't be uttered in polite company or in front of impressionable minds. There are no civilized words that can neutralize the obscenity of the indignity.

Papa Corn pulls out his veiny pecker and shoves it into the severed-head's new cunt-mouth. He pumps and he grunts.

"No teeth baby!"

Unlike Don (and Brandon), the other clowns are quite enjoying the show.

"Talk about a vagina dentata!"

Mister Blister, Noodledome, and Jumbo clap, hoot, and cut some rugs. They've always been impressed by Papa's depravity, but he's reaching new heights tonight.

Papa Corn starts to quiver. His ass-cheeks clench. He tilts his head back and groans, releasing a cum-gusher.

The clowns give him a round of applause.

Papa pulls out. He regards Tiffany's head for a moment. Then he tosses it into a trashcan.

"She wasn't that good."

CHAPTER 18

MALAS NOTICIAS (BAD NEWS)

Pepe the Mime bursts back into the Clown Trailer having just thrilled everyone under the Big Top with his dangerously insane juggling abilities. The motor on his chainsaw sputters to a halt. He regards Don for a second, sharp metal teeth glistening, before sliding back into the murky recesses of the labyrinth.

Moments later, someone comes knocking.

"Clowns, five minutes. Five minutes, clowns!"

Don watches as a cigarette-smoking Mister Blister unstraps Brandon from the chair and yanks him by the collar.

"It's showtime, shit-face."

Mister Blister drags a stumbling Brandon out the door and down Clown Alley. Papa Corn follows close behind.

"See you again soon, Donald," he promises.

On his way out, Jumbo stops to show Don his new pig

puppet. There's just enough time for a quick game of Toesies. His puppet pokes Don's bare feet.

"This little piggy went to market..." he says in a squeaky voice. "This little piggy stayed home. This little piggy had roast beef. This little piggy had none..." Jumbo's voice somehow drops impossibly low. "And this little piggy went wee-wee-wee all the way home!"

Noodledome's the last out the door. He finishes packing up his tools, closes his Kung-Fu lunchbox, and lays a moist dirty towel over Tiffany's severed head. (Obviously, he pulled it out of the trashcan after Papa was "finished" with her.) He pulls up his baggy Kop pants, grabs his Billy Club, and shuffles out the door.

Don finds himself unsupervised for the first time since his arrival. He strains against his straps and tries to cough out the bloody undies in his mouth, but neither budge. When he cranes his neck around, he's barely able to see a crappy TV set.

The little girl's on the couch watching the news. She's sitting next to a little boy with balloons tied to his wrists, a bowl of goldfish in his lap.

The little boy isn't moving.

The "MURDER IN TEXAS" graphic fills the entire TV screen before shrinking into an insert window next to Angela Maverick's head and chest.

"We have the very latest on a story out of Odessa. Two people... dead. Three people... missing. Two of them... young girls."

Don can't believe it! She's talking about his wife and daughters!

"And now we have just learned the identity of the two dead. One is a local police officer, twenty-eight-year-old Thomas Dwayne Carter."

A heroic portrait of T.C. in uniform fills the screen.

"Thomas was a decorated lawman and a six-year veteran of the police force. The second victim is thirty-five-year-old Tiffany Sinclair-Johnson."

T.C.'s portrait switches to a glamor photo of Tiffany.

Don moans.

"Tiffany is the mother of the two missing girls: fourteen-year-old Alyssa and ten-year-old Hillary Johnson."

The glamor photo of Tiffany switches to a candid photo of Alyssa and Hillary with their arms around each other's shoulders.

Don groans. He's shook. Tears stream down his face.

"Police are looking for these two young girls as well as their father, Donald Arthur Johnson." Don perks up. This means they're trying to rescue him too!

The photo of the kids switches to an unflattering photo of Don frozen in a half-smile, looking like a dipshit. "Police aren't calling him a suspect yet, but he is a person of interest."

Don can't believe it! They think *he* did it? He's beside himself, incensed that they could even think him capable of killing his wife!"

"Officers speculate that his reappearance could lead to the whereabouts of his missing children."

Don's mind races.

Alyssa! Hillary! Where are they?

Don's been so caught up in his own hopeless misery he hadn't yet considered what hell his daughters might be suffering. He imagines the possible horrors and his achy heart breaks all over again.

And with the pain comes fury.

CHAPTER 19

JUEGO ENCENDIDO (GAME ON)

The Clown Trailer door swings open.

Papa Corn and the boys have just completed another successful rendition of their Keystone Kops routine.

The key to a great act is spontaneity. This time, the prisoner clown, Brandon, attempted to "escape" before Noodledome dragged him back out from under the bleachers. The crowd leapt to their feet, tickled pink.

"Wonderful improvisation tonight," Papa Corn praises drugged/unconscious Brandon as Mister Blister puts him into a storage closet. "Wonderful moxie. Wonderful gumption!"

Mister Blister, Noodledome, and Jumbo plop down on the couch with the kids to relax. Pepe the Mime slinks down a hallway with three more chainsaws over his shoulder.

Don hears Papa Corn creeping closer. And he can feel it, Papa's evil energy. He shudders when the head clown pulls up a chair and sits down in front of him.

"Marvelous crowd tonight, Donald," Papa Corn recounts. "Marvelous show. I wish you could have seen it." He switches into his exaggerated happy clown voice and quotes himself: "Shall I use the prod?" He laughs as Don fumes.

"No need to seethe, Donald," Papa Corn says, returning to his mad genius voice. Papa uses wire cutters to remove the bailing wire from around Don's mouth and head.

Noodledome's undies are so saturated with saliva, blood, and bile, they fall out of Don's mouth and land on the floor with a stomach-churning splat.

"Now, Donald. You and I must talk."

It takes a bit for Don to regain the use of his tongue. Papa Corns pours a glass of water cut with urine into his mouth. Don tries to swallow but can only choke and gargle.

"Try it now."

"Where are my girls?" Don yells. These are the first words he's spoken in hours (how many, he has no way of knowing), and his tongue stings with every syllable. "Are they okay?"

"Your daughters, Donald?" Papa Corn replies with more than just a hint of perversion. "Yes... and what delicious girls they are."

"You sick fuck! If you laid one hand on my girls, I swear to God..."

"Relax, Donald." Papa Corn interrupts him. "Your daughters are fine... at least for the time being. But that's where things can get a little tricky."

"I'll do anything!" Don pleads. "Just please, don't hurt them."

"Good, very good, Donald," Papa Corn replies. "That's exactly what I wanted to hear. All you have to do is... everything I say."

Don wonders if it's already too late.

"I wanna see them first," he bargains. "How do I know they're okay?"

"Good question."

"Are they in here?" Don asks, imagining them trapped in one of the trailer's darkest vestibules.

"Afraid not," Papa Corn replies. "They're with The Babysitter."

Don's hardly comforted by this assertion.

"Where are they?" he pleads. "When can I see them?"

"Well..." Papa Corn pulls a cell phone from his pocket. "I just happen to have a video postcard here that Daddy's precious little angels made especially for you."

Don's confused.

Papa Corn scrolls through the selection of videos with an index finger.

"Ah, here we go."

Papa Corn walks behind Don and drapes his arm around him. He holds the phone out so Don can see.

The video comes on and off a few times as someone messes with the record feature. Finally rolling, Don sees a nondescript, dirty building and Mister Blister looking straight into the camera, blowing smoke.

"Recording... Stand by... Action!"

Mister Blister turns the camera around to reveal Alyssa and Hillary tied to a couple of rusty chairs. Both of them are crying uncontrollably.

Noodledome stands a few feet in front of them, holding cue cards for the girls to read.

"Stop the goddamn crying and read the fucking cards!" Mister Blister barks from behind the camera.

Alyssa and Hillary shake their heads and continue crying.

"No? Give 'em the stick, Jumbo!"

Jumbo enters the frame. He approaches Don's daughters

with a little girl puppet on one hand, clutching a cattle prod in the other. He pushes a button; the pain-stick clicks and zaps, spitting blue sparks.

"¡Pórtense bien, niñas!" Jumbo cackles. "Spare the rod, spoil the child!"

The tiny psychopath zaps the hell out of Alyssa and Hillary; they scream.

Don moans.

Finally, Alyssa acquiesces and begins nervously reading the cards in Noodledome's hands, stifling her sobs.

"H-hi, Daddy."

Don weeps.

"It's me and Hillary from s-summer camp. We're having b-bunches of fun and making new f friends. Our camp counselors, Noodledome and Jumbo, are having so much f-fun too..." Alyssa breaks down and lowers her head.

Jumbo zaps Alyssa with the cattle prod again.

She screams, composes herself, and does her best to carry on.

"Please, Daddy!" Alyssa glances over at her sister Hillary, still crying irrepressibly. "T-tell Mom we love her and t-to send cookies."

"Daddy!" Hillary screams.

Jumbo proceeds to zap Alyssa and Hillary indiscriminately until both are shrieking like banshees.

Don's eyes are moist, and his face is red. He looks away.

Papa Corn presses STOP and sits back down across from Don.

"You're a lucky man, Donald. You still have two to fight for. Yes?"

Don, saddened beyond bounds, glares at Papa Corn.

"Now listen to me very carefully," Papa Says. "If you do

everything I say, no matter what I say, I *promise* you that you'll see your girls again."

"Why should I believe you?" Don yells.

"You don't have a choice... I hold all the cards!" In his hand, Papa Corn fans out a deck of Loteria cards. "You play the game right and you'll see your daughters again. It's really that simple." Papa leans in closer to Don. "But if you don't play the game, I promise that I'll cut your daughters into a hundred fucking pieces and feed them to Noodledome myself." His icy eyes cut Don like a knife.

Don breaks down.

"Savvy?" Papa Corn asks. "Do we have a deal?"

Don helplessly nods; he's utterly defeated.

"Okay."

And with that single word, Don Johnson signs his pact with the Devil.

Papa Corn Smiles.

"Look, on the bright side: I may be a homicidal serial rapist whose day job just so happens to be a clown, but I'm definitely not a liar. My word is my word is my bond. Clown's Honor!" Papa Corn holds two fingers in the air, making a mockery of the Boy Scouts' salute. "You do what I say when I say, and you'll see your daughters again."

"I understand." Don's slobbering; his nose is dripping snot. "Are they safe?"

"For now, yes," Papa Corn replies. "But if one of us were to unlock a certain box upon our next visit... Well, let's just say we wouldn't want that to happen."

"What's in the box?"

Papa Corn beams like a proud parent.

"Awww, my greatest creation... We recently dubbed him El Muneco, The Doll Boy."

Don doesn't know Doll Boy from Dumbledore, but he knows enough to be terrified for his daughter's lives.

"Enough chit-chat," Papa Corn continues. "Let's play the game. What do ya say? Yes?"

Don nods that he will.

Papa Corn rises gleefully and kisses Don on the forehead. He claps his hands and rubs his palms together. "Gentlemen, start your engines!"

The other clowns gather around, hooting, yapping, and laughing. It's time to celebrate!

Noodledome's taken the head off of "See 'n' Scream Sally" and wired it to a child's toy. He pulls her string.

"The cow goes... moooooo."

"Come, Donald," Papa Corn says as Mister Blister undoes the chair straps. "It's time for you to get into costume."

CHAPTER 20

IR A DAR UN PASEO (GOING FOR A RIDE)

It's late at night. An emerald-green '68 Camaro with racing stripes is barreling down Highway 20.

Mister Blister's behind the wheel, of course, getting off on the engine's powerful vibrations.

Noodledome sits shotgun with See 'n' Scream Sally's head in his lap.

Don's in the back, sandwiched between Papa Corn and Jumbo.

A surprise or two might be hiding in the trunk.

Don's been given his very own prisoner's outfit, complete with striped cap. It's identical to the one Brandon wears, only slightly cleaner. His face has been painted as a traditional sad clown with rosy cheeks and gray stubble.

Papa Corn's flipping through his Loteria cards in a meditative state.

This is the calm before the storm.

Papa Corn got his first deck of Loteria cards from migrants he slaughtered in El Paso. He was a much younger clown back then and quite uncertain about his future. He found himself mesmerized by the characters and objects.

He started imagining scenarios that could connect them all into a single epic story.

While high on Peyote one night, Papa Corn had a vision. The vision came with revelations and pointed his life in a new direction. He knew the perfect way to link all fifty-plus Loteria cards: murder.

One card equals one victim—at least!

Papa Corn's been steadily whittling down his deck of cards for months now, crossing off new victims every time The Big Old Circus puts down stakes.

But if the stars align right, Papa Corn might just get to the bottom of the stack—tonight!

"We need gas," Mister Blister announces.

"Then let's get some," Papa Corn replies.

CHAPTER 21

EL BORRACHO Y LA ROSA
(THE DRUNK AND THE ROSE)

Mister Blister pulls up to a gas pump outside T-Wood Grocery and Beer. He gets out and starts filling the tank. He sees a "No Smoking" sign and scoffs, lighting up a fresh cigarette.

Papa and his clowns also exit the Camaro.

As they do, a Mexican family leaves the convenience store and walks towards their chromed-out pickup truck.

A precocious seven-year-old pauses when she spots the clowns. She waves at Papa Corn before putting her hands on her hips.

Papa Corn waves back, then looks down at his stack of Loteria cards searching for a match.

"¡Vamos, Mi-ha!" her father calls out while opening the doors of their truck.

Mi-ha hurries along and gets into the back seat. As the truck pulls out, she waves to the clowns from the back window.

Papa Corn momentarily laments the loss of such a precious potential victim.

"Too bad," he mutters.

But the night's young!

When the tank's full, Mister Blister yanks Don out of the backseat by his leash ("Let's go, asshole!") and all five of them proceed inside the store. No one knows exactly how things will go down, but in Papa Corn they trust.

A brass cow-bell clank-clanks as they file inside.

Rose Wilcox, the beautiful woman behind the counter, and "Big" Joe Bitterman, the seedy-looking night manager, are immediately taken aback. For a second, they're almost frozen. This certainly isn't something you see every day.

"Whoa, hey," red-headed Rose says with a smile. "Is the circus in town?"

As the others head further inside, Papa Corn stops at the counter and smiles back at Rose. She's struck by his icy blue eyes.

"Can I help you find anything?" Rose asks with a twinge of nervousness.

"Why, yes... Yes, you can," Papa Corn replies, salivary glands tingling.

"And that would be...?"

"Well, now, that depends..." Papa Corn leans in to read her name tag. "Rose."

"On what?"

"Hmm..." Papa Corn's grin widens. The game is afoot, and this is foreplay!

While that's going on, Mister Blister goes to investigate an old arcade game in the corner, dragging Don behind him. He smiles when he sees its one of his old favorites: *Gal Panic*.

A player starts by choosing a hostess. Then, it's basically a puzzle where you avoid things like triangles and spiders while sectioning-off portions of patterns. When the pattern is completely cleared, the hostess returns wearing nothing but her 68-bit birthday suit.

"Sid'down!" Mister Blister shouts at Don.

Like an obedient and broken dog, Don immediately sits and cowers against the side of the machine.

Just do what you're told, he reminds himself. *Whatever it takes to get my daughters back!*

Mister Blister drops a quarter into the slot and chooses his hostess.

"You are Lucky!" a girly digital voice announces. "I'm Nami!"

"Hmm." Mister Blister smiles and his eyes widen as he dives into the gameplay.

"Oh, feels good!" Nami assures him.

Simultaneously, Jumbo makes a beeline towards the store's tiny toy section: a small wall of cheap plastic knock offs. He and his pig puppet both seem overjoyed. He tears open a pack of slinky eyes, slaps them on his face, and yips with delight.

Night manager Big Joe, fat with white hair and a goatee, takes it all in as he finishes stocking a shelf with snack cakes. Something's not right, he can already tell. He decides to head into the back office, where he can watch them on the security monitors.

When he turns around, however, he comes belly to belly Noodledome, who's eating a large bag of potato chips.

"Hi. Can I help you?" Big Joe asks.

Noodledome replies with a silent smile, still chewing chips.

"Do you need some help?" Big Joe asks again, clearly uneasy.

Noodledome's smile widens as he continues devouring potato chips, but he says nothing.

"Okay then." Big Joe slowly backs away toward the stockroom. "Well, just let me know if I can help you with anything."

At the counter, Papa Corn continues softening Rose. At this point, she's comfortable enough to tell him personal things about herself.

"You know," she reveals, "my brother is deathly afraid of clowns."

"Is that a fact?" Papa Replies, suppressing drool.

"Yep," she continues. "Ever since we were young, anytime he sees a clown, he freaks out. I think there's a word for that, right?"

"Yes, there's a technical term for that," Papa tells her. "It's called quit-being-a-bitch-a-citus."

"That's funny!" Rose giggles. "I'll make sure and tell him that the next time I see him." Rose twirls a section of her hair with her finger. "Wanna see my rose tattoo?"

Papa practically gushes.

She turns around and leans forward to show off her tramp-stamp.

Papa Corn searches his cards until he finds La Rosa—The Rose. It's too perfect.

Rose turns back around and sees the colorful card.

"What's that?" she asks. "A Tarot Card?"

"No," Papa Corn grins. "It's a simple card game. Kind of like Bingo, but from Mexico." Papa takes on a seductive tenor. "Now, this particular card happens to be the La Rosa card. It means, 'The beauty of the Rose.'"

Rose blushes.

"I love roses—obviously!"

"Yes, I definitely noticed," Papa Corn replies. "Unfortunately, that's not a good thing."

"Why's that?" Rose asks, slightly unnerved.

Papa Corn whistles to get the attention of his partners and flashes the La Rosa card.

They look up and nod.

Papa Corn's ready to pounce, but he's interrupted by the clank-clank of the cowbell.

"Well dip me in shit and fry me in batter!" It's "Pa" Skullit, the neighborhood booze hound. "Well ain't this somthin'!... Hello darlin'!" He tips his hat to Rose on his way back to the beer aisle.

"We call him Pa Skullit because of his hairstyle," Rose tells Papa. "You know? Like a mullet? Bald on top, party in the back!"

"You don't say?" Papa Corn replies.

Part of being a great showman is being able to improvise on the fly.

Papa Corn flips through his stack of cards.

"Oh, Noodledome!" Papa turns and flashes the El Borracho—The Drunkard Loteria card.

Noodledome nods and follows Pa to the beer aisle.

"What's that about?" Rose asks.

"Nothing that's going to matter to you in about 30 seconds."

Pa pulls a six-pack of Pabst from the rack. He turns to head back to the counter, but he's blocked by Noodledome.

"Well, howdy there! You're a big un, huh, Hoss?"

Noodledome smiles as he pulls his mallet from its back holster.

"Well, fuck ya very much!"

Noodledome smashes Pa square in the chest with the mallet.

Pa flies back with such force his body shatters a few glass doors. Bottles and cans pour out, crashing across the floor, spraying foam.

Noodledome bursts into a fit of his signature insane laughter before delivering the kill-smash. Pa's head busts open like a cantaloupe.

"What's going on?" Rose asks, alarmed.

Papa Corn jumps over the counter and approaches the trembling Rose.

"Rose, we have never seen a plant that we would not cut down, or a person alive, we would not plant in the ground..."

"W-what do you want? Are you gonna rob me?"

"Yesss," Papa Corn replies like a serpent, licking his lips and massaging his crotch. "But I don't want your money."

He pushes Rose to the floor.

She watches in fear as Papa Corn throws off his jacket and loses his suspenders. His pants fall to the floor. She screams.

"It gets what it wants," Papa says.

Rose's eyes fill with terror.

The head of Papa Corn's circumcised penis is painted up in clown-face.

"Last clown in is a rotten egg!" comes a squeaky, cartoon voice. Papa Corn uses his fingers to open and close the opening of his urethra like tiny lips. "I get what I want!"

Papa pounces.

Don sees what's happening, and it's tearing him up inside, but he's powerless to intervene.

Suddenly, Big Joe bursts through the stockroom doors with a pump-action shotgun, yelling and firing wildly like Rambo. Glass breaks, plaster cracks, and products are shredded. But none of the clowns are hit.

"Oh, shit!" Big Joe says when he runs out of shots.

From the top of a shelf, Jumbo jumps onto Joe's shoulders, snorting like a pig.

"¡Lo arruinaste!" he screams, tearing at the night manager's eyeballs.

Joe hollers, drops the gun, and tries to buck Jumbo off his back like a bronco.

But the little clown holds tight. Oinking and cackling, Jumbo presses his pig puppet against Joe's temple and fires the gun hidden inside twice. Joe's brains fly everywhere as his body crumples.

As Joe twitches on the floor, Jumbo steals his shotgun and scurries toward the stockroom (to steal the security tapes and any additional ammo). While pilfering, he finds a stack of pictures that Big Joe's voyeur ass took of Rose while using the bathroom.

While Papa Corn continues violating Rose behind the counter, Mister Blister's making serious headway of his own on *Gal Panic*.

"You are sweet!" Nami coos.

"Thank you, baby," Mister Blister replies. "Very nice, very nice." He imagines turning naked Nami inside-out like a sock-puppet.

Noodledome plops down in the beer aisle to eat some snack-cakes dipped in Pa's blood and brain matter.

Don's in shock.

Finished with Rose, Papa Corn rises from behind the counter while pulling up his pants. Naked and bleeding, Rose attempts a daring escape by hopping over the counter. Papa grabs her by her ankle and pulls her back.

"Nine, nine, fräulein!" he says while smacking her tushy. "Dirty whore!" He pulls her back behind the counter. "Guess what, Rose? It's time for the money shot."

Papa Corn grabs a devastated Rose by her hair and drags her out from behind the counter. He pushes her into the front of the counter, up against a banner for a zombie-themed draft beer. He holds her wrists down with his feet and fondles her body.

"Mister Noodledome, please bring Donald over here."

Noodledome drags Don from Mister Blister's side over to the checkout counter.

Don looks bewildered as Papa Corn puts T.C.'s gun into his hands and forces him to point it at a panic-stricken Rose.

"Wanna see your daughters again?" Papa asks.

"Y...yes, I do!" Don replies

"Then kill this bitch."

Rose immediately starts to plead for her life.

Don's eyes widened in terror.

"Take this gun, put it in her mouth, and pull the trigger," Papa hisses.

"I can't do that," Don whines. "I don't wanna hurt anyone."

"Donald, I won't ask you again. Rose here is dead. But your girls don't have to be. It's your choice."

Don's never felt more conflicted—few have.

"Please don't make me!"

"I'm not making you do anything," Papa replies. "You're choosing this because you love your daughters more than Rose here."

Don blubbers.

"Since it's your first time," Papa Corn says. "I'll give you a hand." He places Don's finger on the trigger and holds it in place with his own finger. "Now, Rose, I want you to open your mouth and say, ah!"

Papa forces Don to put the barrel of the gun into a Rose's reluctant mouth.

Rose's teeth chatter against the metal barrel.

"Relax your elbow," Papa Corn instructs. "This feels good, doesn't it? You hold her precious life in your hands. What do you say, Donald? Let's play God."

"Stop," Don cries. "Please. Stop!"

"Hollow point tuck in hollow head, spin a bedtime story that awakens the dead!"

Don and Papa Corn pull the trigger. Rose's head explodes, covering them in blood and brains. Papa Corn licks his lips as Donald crumples to the ground, psychologically depleted.

"I'm sorry," Don mutters, hoping Rose can forgive him from the Afterlife. "I'm so sorry."

"She can't hear you, Donald. She's dead!" Papa corn leans in and French-kisses Rose's pulped face.

"Game over!" Nami announces.

"It's time to go!" Papa rallies his troops. "Take what you want!"

On the way out, Jumbo hands Big Joe's shotgun to Mister Blister, who admires it.

Noodledome picks up Rose's body and effortlessly throws her over his shoulder like a large bag of dog food.

Papa Corn leaves T.C.'s gun behind on the counter—on purpose.

CHAPTER 22

MONTAJE (MONTAGE)

It's already been a ratings boon for the News 7 team, and things are only getting grislier. Viewers across West Texas are tuning in for more hard-hitting reporting.

The "MURDER IN TEXAS" graphic takes up the entire screen before shrinking into an insert window next to Angela Maverick's head.

"Still no word on the whereabouts of Alyssa, Hillary, or their father Donald Johnson," she tells her viewers. "If you have any information regarding his whereabouts, please call the police immediately."

As the emerald-green Camaro peels out and departs the parking lot of T-Wood Grocery and Beer, Papa Corns looks down at his shrinking pile of Loteria cards. There are only a handful left. He decides they're gonna go for it!

They set out on a psychedelic, psychopathic orgy of savagery. A fever dream of bone-crushing afflictions and bloody havoc. Fueled by amphetamine and insanity, Papa predicts a kill spree unlike anything anyone's ever seen!

And how fulfilled they'll all feel when that deck of cards finally whittles down to nothing. Papa Corn will be a legend, earning himself a seat in the front Antrum of Hell between Lucifer and Baphomet. No one in West Texas will ever forget *this* time The Big Old Circus came to town!

The bodies stack up fast!

In Don's fractured mind, it all becomes a blur.

La Dama—The Lady: Papa Corn leans out the back window and shoots the first random bitch he sees. Mister Blister stops the car so Noodledome can pick her up and throw her in the trunk.

El Cerebro—The Brain: Mister Blister runs a man down, then backs up over his head, crushing it like a honeydew.

El-Calavera—The Skull: Noodledome scalps a bald man, peeling away the skin on his head while Mister Blister and Jumbo hold him down.

Across Texas, people are glued to their seats, watching the news.

Angela Maverick's on fire.

"As violence plagues our street, there is now a statewide manhunt in effect for Donald Arthur Johnson, who is considered to be armed and extremely dangerous."

The same unflattering photo of Don fills the screen.

"If you have any information about the whereabouts of this man, please call 911 immediately!"

At the end of a quiet, residential cul-de-sac, Conway-Twitty-Hating Gene Jenkins is yelling at his TV from the comfort of his tattered recliner.

"Pussy!" he yells at the picture of Don looking like a dipshit, shaking his fist.

There's a huge American Flag hanging on his wall. His

medals are on display, as are framed photos of a twenty-five-year-old Gene in uniform. Pictures and tchotchkes immortalizing John Wayne make it clear that the octogenarian is quite a fan of classic westerns.

Without warning, BAM! Gene's front door is kicked off its hinges.

Mister Blister strolls in carrying Joe's shotgun, followed by Papa Corn, Noodledome, Jumbo, and a reluctant Don.

The TV continues playing as Gene sizes up the intruders.

"What in tarnation do you fuckers want?" he sneers. "God damn pussy clowns!"

Papa Corn flashes El Soldado—The Soldier card.

Mister Blister blows a smoke cloud as he pulls the shotgun's trigger.

Gene's chest explodes as his entire chair falls backward, leaving the man's feet pointed at the ceiling.

And on it goes, this onslaught of brutality, this psycho-sadistic road-trip into oblivion, this crazy runaway freight train going off its rails.

The clowns pull victims behind dumpsters, into abandoned storefronts, and down dark alleys.

Don loses time and comes to, horrified, to find a bloody hacksaw in one hand and a severed arm in the other. Did he do this? He notices the spider tattoo on the arm as Papa Corn flashes Vueda Negra—The Black Widow.

He comes around again holding an AR-15. The rifle's muzzle is duct-taped into a brawny man's mouth. He represents the El Valiente card, The Brave Man. Papa Corn forces Don to pull the trigger—or maybe he did it on his own this time. He can't tell anymore.

Don finds himself sitting in an alley with a dead woman's head in his lap. Her stomach's been ripped open. She has La Madre—The Mother card stapled to her forehead.

"I'm sorry," Don weeps as he strokes her long dark hair.

"She can't hear you, Don!" Papa Corn taunts. "She's dead! Dead! She's fucking dead!"

Noodledome swings a fetus around by its umbilical cord, laughing powerfully. He brings the underbaked baby down hard onto the pavement, turning it to mush.

It's candy for Papa Corn's eyes and ears.

Mister Blister smokes and slashes.

Noodledome's got more female flesh in the trunk than he knows what to do with.

Jumbo and his menagerie of puppets have never felt more alive.

And on they go.

In an abandoned dog-housein the oil fields, Alyssa and Hillary are gagged and bound. They stare, petrified, at a huge industrial-sized refrigerator, wrapped in chains, just feet away. They weren't sure at first, but now they know it's true: There's something terrible inside.

It has a hammer!

Angela Maverick keeps the populus informed with up to the minute coverage.

"Police seem overwhelmed by a grisly murder scene inside the T-Wood grocery store. Here's Linda Ito on location."

The streams switch. Linda's standing right outside T-Wood's. There are several cop cars in the lot, an ambulance, and police tape everywhere. Officers dart around half-dazed.

"That's right, Angela," Linda takes over. "Police say the gruesome attacks took place around eleven pm at the T-Wood on West 42nd Street. Police are uncertain if this crime is linked to the recent attack of the Johnson family..."

That same unflattering picture of Don fills the screen. Fucking dipshit.

Behind Linda, a cop comes running out of the T-Wood, puking all over himself.

CHAPTER 23

EL ARMA (THE GUN)

"God dammit, Deacon! That's twice in one night!"

Detective Roper returns to surveying the extensive damage inside T-Wood's.

If Don Johnson did this, then he must be on some new-fangled hardcore PCP, he thinks. It boggles his mind.

Officer Goodson calls him over.

"Sir, look at this."

Detective Roper carefully walks toward the front counter. It's almost impossible not to step in evidence, but he tries his best to keep his cowboy boots clean.

"What is it? Let me guess. More blood?"

"Yeah, that, but lots of skull and brain matter, too."

Detective Roper looks closer.

"Somebody got shot here," he quickly deduces. "Point blank range."

"So, where's the body?" Officer Goodson asks.

"That's a good question, but... Hello, what do we have here?"

Roper notices the gun Papa Corn left on the counter.

"You thinking what I'm thinking?" Officer Goodson asks.

"I am indeed. That's gotta be T.C.'s gun."

"There's our link to Don Johnson," Officer Goodson reckons. "He took T.C.'s gun after he killed him, then came here and shot up the place."

"And Bingo was his name-o," Detective Roper replies. "Let's get the word out."

CHAPTER 24

EL MURANO (THE PIG)

The emerald-green '68 Camaro is now a literal vehicle of destruction. The clowns speed back and forth across Highway 20 between Odessa and Midland, leaving trails of blood, tears, and body parts in their wake.

How long has this been happening? Don wonders, drifting in and out of consciousness in the backseat. Has this really just been one ultra-violent night, or has this depravity been spiraling out of control for weeks? He can't tell anymore.

Heavy Southern rock blasts as the Camaro barrels past a speed-trap. A highway patrol car peels out in pursuit, lights flashing, siren wailing.

Mister Blister checks the rearview mirror and turns down the radio.

"It's the fuzz," he reports, clenching his cigarette between his teeth.

Papa Corn turns to Don and sticks a knife up against his side.

"Think about your daughters, Donald."

Don stares directly into Papa Corn's eyes.

"I've done everything you've asked so far," Don replies with shame and venom. "Why would I try something now?"

"Good," Papa Corn replies, slapping Don on the cheek. "Just remember, if this goes south, no one will ever find Alyssa and Hillary. Do you understand?"

"I understand."

The Camaro pulls off the highway, makes a few random turns, and parks across from The Ector Theater on North Texas Avenue. The venue's closing up for the night after a special one night only double-feature screening of *Jaws* and *The Texas Chainsaw Massacre.*

"You've come a long way, Donald," Papa Corn says with a smile. "You don't have much further to go now."

The patrol car comes to a stop behind the Camaro.

The driver's door opens, and Deputy Bradley Potts exits the vehicle. He approaches the muscle car using standard protocols. He pulls his pants up by his gun belt and spits.

Now, just because Deputy Potts is a laughingstock (a modern reincarnation of Sheriff Buford T. Justice) that doesn't mean he can be fucked with. He'd been a drill sergeant before joining the force and, even though most lawmen his age worked desk jobs, he simply loves patrolling the highways at night.

He's less than a week away from early retirement.

Deputy Potts approaches the driver's side window of the Camaro, leans down, and shines his flashlight into the dark car.

"You gotta be bullshitting me," he says out loud before spitting.

"Good evening, officer," Mister Blister says through the open window. He's doing his darndest to don a friendly smile, clutching his cigarette between his teeth.

"Good evening," Deputy Potts replies, still sizing up the situation. "I'm guessing the circus is in town?" he says sarcastically.

"Yes, sir. Present and accounted for." Blister says.

"What are y'all doing way out here so late?" Deputy Potts inquires.

"We figured it was a nice night for a drive, Officer." Mister Blister smiles directly into Deputy Potts' flashlight, barely squinting.

"I guess it—"

Deputy Potts is interrupted by a car racing by. Decorated in the colors of a local high school, its teenage occupants are hooting and hollering as the driver leans on his horn. Their football team, Ector Fighting Chupacabras, won tonight, putting them one win away from being crowned district champs.

Deputy Potts's uniform flaps in the wake, nearly knocking his cowboy hat off.

Harassing Deputy Potts was something of a local pastime. These kids' parents did it, as well as their aunts and uncles.

"Goddamnit!" he hollers while shaking his fist. "Fucking punk kids!"

Deputy Potts stares daggers as the teenagers' taillights fade. He shakes his head and turns his attention back to the clowns.

"Alright, let me go ahead and see your driver's license and proof of insurance, please."

"Sure thing," Mister Blister replies as he pulls a stolen wallet out of his back pocket. He finds a driver's license and hands it over.

As Deputy Potts shines a light on the license, Noodledome opens the glove compartment to find the insurance card. Brandon's severed hand, still wearing the knock-off Rolex, falls out. He swiftly kicks it under his seat before finding the insurance card.

As Deputy Potts looks things over, Papa Corn shuffles through his dwindling deck of Loteria cards. He whistles softly to his crew as he flashes El Murano—The Pig.

Deputy Potts leans down to compare Mister Blister to the photo on the license.

"Alright, Mr.... Clapp. I'm going to assume that's you under all that shit on your face?"

"Yes, sir," Mister Blister responds, cool as a frozen margarita. "Indeed, it is."

Deputy Potts looks back at the license, still not 100% convinced.

"Well, just how many clowns are in this car tonight, Mr. Clapp?"

"Let's see..." Mister Blister thinks about it for a moment. "Four?"

"Well, since you don't sound sure of yourself, let's do a quick head count, shall we?" Deputy Potts shines his light on Mister Blister. "There's one." When he shines his light on Noodledome, the large clown waves and smiles. "That's two." The light shines on Papa Corn, who stares back in silence. "Three." Finally, he shines on Don, who looks away in fear and shame. "And four. Is that it?"

"Yes sir," Mister Blister smiles. "The rest of 'em had the night off, officer."

"I see."

A crackling/whirring sound accompanied by a female voice comes from somewhere inside the car.

"The pig goes: Oink-oink-oink!"

It's See 'n' Scream Sally.She's been riding along with the boys this whole time.

A baffled Deputy Potts looks over at Noodledome, who's simply smiling. The lawman's eyes narrow and his lips tighten.

"Y'all got something to say?" Deputy Potts sneers at the clowns, all shaking their heads, attempting to look innocent. "No? Good. In that case—"

"The pig goes: Oink-oink-oink!" See 'n' Scream Sally just can't help herself. Simply irrepressible!

Deputy Potts's face turns red.

"Alright, that's it. I want all of you to exit the vehicle now. Now!"

"Something wrong, officer?" Mister Blister feigns ignorance and surprise.

"Just step out of the vehicle, Mr. Clapp. All of you. Move ladies!"

"Yes sir," Mister Blister replies and complies. The rest of the car's occupants follow suit.

"Think about your girls," Papa Corn reminds Don as he exits the Camaro.

Jumbo, previously unnoticed by Deputy Potts, covertly slips out of the backseat undetected.

Simultaneously, another car full of rowdy disrespectful teenagers from the football game races by, ruffling Deputy Potts with its wake.

Deputy Potts shakes his fist as he watches the car speed away.

"God damn you little bastards!" He turns back to the clowns. "Okay, everybody, line up."

While this scene plays out, Jumbo creeps into Deputy Potts's patrol car. He spots a large shotgun attached to the dashboard that happens to be unlocked. He looks at his small revolver and decides to level up, trading his pea-shooter for a boom-stick. He cocks the pump.

"Alright," Potts continues humorlessly. "Y'all have a seat right there on the sidewalk. I'm gonna check a few things out."

If any of the clowns are nervous, they don't show it.

Donald, on the other hand, has a pit the size of a football in his guts.

Will this be it? He wonders. *Will the cop call for back-up? Will this end in a hail of gunfire and, if so, what will happen to Alyssa and Hillary?*

Deputy Potts returns to his squad car and opens the driver's door. He's startled to find a small clown pointing his own shotgun at him. There's no time to react.

Jumbo blasts Deputy Potts in his face.

The force sends the Deputy reeling, blood spurting, chunks of flesh flying. He stumbles backward into the street and right into the path of a speeding SUV filled with teenagers. The cop's body is obliterated like a goblin in a microwave.

For a moment, the clowns watch in calm disbelief.

Papa Corn breaks the stunned silence.

"Gentlemen," he says. "Let's improvise!"

CHAPTER 25

CHUPACABRAS DE LA ESCUELA SECUNDARIA ECTOR (THE ECTOR HIGH SCHOOL CHUPACABRAS)

"I swear to God, you guys. He's the scariest clown ever!"

That's Kirk. He's behind the wheel of his father's SUV with an optional third row of seats. Plenty of room for all of his friends.

"Scarier than Pennywise?" Pam asks. She's sitting shotgun.

"Way!" Kirk assures her.

Teenagers Kirk, Pam, Jerry, Sally, Kim, and Franklin have been driving around aimlessly for hours (ever since the football game ended), drinking beer and smoking skunk-weed.

"What's this clown's name?" Jerry asks from the second row.

"Art!"

"That's not a very scary name, Kirk," Sally says from all the way in the back.

"You have no idea!" Kirk replies.

"I have to pee," Franklin complains from the third row.

"What makes him so fucking scary?" Kim asks from the second row.

"He saws a woman completely in half!" Kirk replies. "Starting at her vee-jay!"

"Spoilers!" Jerry complains.

"That's the most disgusting thing I've ever heard of!" Pam says.

"You think that's bad? He also rubs shit all over the..." Kirk's cut off.

Without warning, the SUV plows straight into Deputy Potts. The policeman explodes across the windshield, the hood, the grill, the roof, the bumper... you get the point.

Everyone screams as Kirk slams on the brakes.

"What the fuck!" he yells.

"Jesus Christ, what did you do?" distraught Pam asks.

"He jumped out in front of me!" Kirk explains. "Shit! What do I do?"

"I might throw-up," Franklin says.

"Holy shit, man!" Jerry's shaken. "This is really bad, man."

"Someone check on him!" Sally screams.

"Check on what?" Kim hollers. "There's no way he's alive!"

"But we have to check!" Pam replies.

Kirk turns off the SUV and removes the keys from the ignition.

The teens brace themselves for the worst as they get out to examine the horrible scene. As the brave ones venture forward, scaredy-Franklin, his t-shirt sporting a smiley face with a bullet hole in its forehead, stays close to the SUV.

"Fuck me, man," Franklin mutters, shaking his head. "We're all drunk, and we just killed a cop. We're definitely going to jail for this. I'm way too soft for jail!" He pushes a dozen empty beer bottles under the back seats.

Kirk, Pam, Sally, Kim, and Jerry view the carnage. It's overwhelming.

Only now do they notice the row of deadpan clowns standing in front of a police car and a green Camaro.

"What the hell is going on?" Kirk asks the eerily silent spectators. "Did y'all call for help?"

"Kirk, what's happening?" Franklin calls from the SUV.

"I don't know," Kirk calls back. "There's a bunch of clowns over here."

"Did you say clowns?"

"I think so..."

"Now I really have to pee," Franklin says.

"It's okay!" Papa Corn calls out with a smile, waving them forward. "It's all under control here."

"Did you call the cops?" a freaked-out Kirk asks.

"I've called the police and they're on their way," Papa Corn assures them. "Everything is going to be capital A-okay."

Kirk seems even more confused, but keeps walking closer, sheepishly followed by the others.

Papa Corn flashes the okay sign with his left hand. His right hand reaches into his jacket to retrieve his .45 automatic, smile never faltering.

Alarmed, Kirk stops in his tracks.

"Hey, what are you doing?"

Papa Corn blasts him in the chest.

Kirk falls back onto the street gasping, his blood now mixing with the remnants of Deputy Potts.

Pam, Sally, Kim, and Jerry are beyond shocked.

"Oh my God!" Sally screams.

"Kirk!" Pam screams.

As Kirk lies in the street, bleeding profusely from a hole in his sternum, Papa walks over and steps on Kirk's left hand, preventing him from reaching the SUV's keys.

Papa looks down at Kirk, his smile turning dark.

"Tell 'em Papa sent ya!"

This guy's definitely scarier than Art the Clown, is Kirk's final thought before Papa Corn blasts his head all over the asphalt.

Everyone's frozen—paralyzed. Is this really happening?

The clowns take a few steps towards the teens, pulling dismayed Don along by his collar.

It's a standoff in front of The Ector Theater. But it doesn't last long.

Papa Corn opens his arms, as if offering them a big old group hug.

"It's showtime!" he screams in his exaggerated, over-the-top clown voice.

Nope.

Pam, Sally, Kim, and Jerry scream and scatter.

The clowns descend.

Noodledome clobbers Pam before she can sprint away. He drags her, kicking and screaming, over to the back of the Camaro and pops open the trunk.

Pam can hardly comprehend the sheer volume of bodies and body parts inside. There clearly isn't room, but Noodledome *makes* room, cramming her in and slamming the trunk down on her cranium.

Seeing this, cowardly Franklin hops behind the wheel of the Kirk's dad's SUV, fully intent on abandoning his friends and getting the fuck out of there. But, oh shit, where are the keys? Kirk must have taken them with him!

"Fuck!" he screams, bailing out, ready to run for his life. Instead, he finds himself standing nearly chest to chest with Mister Blister.

Franklin lets out a womanly scream.

Mister Blister looks down at the teen's smiley-face-with-bullet-hole t-shirt.

"Irony," he smirks, blowing a cloud of smoke. Mister Blister aims his pistol at Jerry's forehead and pulls the trigger.

Papa Corn calmly raises his whistle, puts it to his painted lips, and blows.

On cue, Pepe the Chainsaw Juggling Mime springs out of the trunk of the Camaro where he's been hiding the entire time (as clowns are adept at doing).

He fires up the biggest, loudest, scariest dragster chainsaw anybody's ever seen. The beast's name is Minnie Pearl, and she's got "HOWDY" carved into her oversized guide bar.

Instinctively, Pepe rushes towards Sally, Kim, and Jerry, who all seem to be making a beeline towards the entrance of The Ector Theater.

In a case of tragic serendipity, an employee of The Ector opens the doors to take out some bags of trash. From a distance, Mister Blister puts a bullet in his brain before he can even start to comprehend the situation.

"Wrong place, wrong time, shithead," Mister Blister says while lighting up a fresh cigarette.

Flight mode on overdrive, Sally and Jerry hop over the dead Ector employee's body and straight inside.

Kim, unfortunately, trips over the fresh corpse and falls on her face. When she peers up, she's looking into the eyes of a very ugly, very small clown. He's holding a roll of duct-tape in his right hand.

"No pelees, querida," Jumbo yaps. "No te haré daño. We want to save you for later!"

Kim screams as Jumbo tackles her and swiftly incapacitates her with duct-tape.

Simultaneously, Pepe the Mime charges past with his chainsaw blazing, following Jerry and Sally into The Ector.

"Gentlemen!" Papa Corn brings his soldiers to attention. "Erase the evidence!"

Noodledome grabs duct-taped Kim and crams her, hardly willingly, into the trunk with the others.

Jumbo hops into the police car and drives off recklessly (his feet barely reach the pedals).

Mister Blister pushes the teens' SUV off the road.

"Mister Blister, when you're done there, I'd like you and Noodledome to bring the Camero around to the back of the theater."

Mister Blister replies to Papa Corn's orders with a blink of the eyes and a cloud of cigarette smoke

"What do you say, Donald?" Papa Corn asks, literally yanking his chain. "Let's see a movie!"

Don can already hear Pepe demolishing the theater from the inside with his incredible chainsaw. He doesn't want to go in there. How much more can one man take? But like everything else that's transpired tonight, Don doesn't have a choice.

Papa Corn smiles.

"Donald... I sure hope it's a love story."

CHAPTER 26

NOCHE DE PELÍCULA (MOVIE NIGHT)

Back in its heyday, The Ector Theater was considered a spectacular example of the Art Moderne aesthetic. The single-screen theater's known for its orange brickwork, green granite, and a neon marquee that wraps all the way around a corner. Founded in 1951, The Ector featured decades of Hollywood's best until it shuttered in 1985.

A period of inactivity and deterioration followed until a non-profit called Friends of The Ector Theater launched in 2001 to oversee the historic landmark's restoration and reopening. With 756 fixed seats, The Ector Theater remains a premier venue for films, plays, concerts, and workshops to this day.

Of course, they're going to need to close for repairs for a while after what happens tonight.

At Papa Corn's behest, Pepe, the Chainsaw Juggling Mime, follows Jerry and Sally into The Ector. He bursts through the doors with his humongous chainsaw blaring and belching blue smoke. He sees the teens heading into the main auditorium and charges at them, destroying the venue's expensive carpets, wood-paneling, and the concession stand as he goes.

Jerry and Sally duck down behind a row of empty seats to hide. They take a moment to gather their wits and catch their breath.

"When I say run," Jerry whispers, heaving, "I want you to run."

"Okay," Sally replied with frightened eyes.

"Whatever happens," he continues, "don't stop."

"What do you mean?" she cries, confused.

They can hear Pepe's chainsaw closing in. He's in the room with them now!

"Whatever happens, keep running!" Jerry commands. "Now run!"

As Sally bolts up front to find a back exit, Jerry stands up and waves his arm.

"Hey, Trap-jaw! I'm over here!" he screams.

Pepe has him in his sights.

"Come and get me, goddamn it!"

It's a heroic thing Jerry's doing: giving Sally a chance to escape. They aren't even boyfriend/girlfriend. He's just a young man with a lot of integrity and balls of steel. There have been plenty of characters with low moral standing in this saga, but Jerry isn't one of them.

Pepe charges.

Jerry's not quiet about it, but he doesn't even look away as Pepe sticks Minnie between the teenager's legs and proceeds to chainsaw him completely in half.

Jerry lets out a guttural wail as his bones and organs shatter and shred. But soon, the only sound that remains is Pepe's insatiable chainsaw, still hungry for more flesh.

In near darkness, Sally runs behind the curtain and backstage. It's a maze of dressing rooms and storage rooms, offices and dead ends. She's frantic! She sees a sign for the loading dock and follows it, desperate for egress.

She finds a set of double doors beneath a red EXIT sign. She makes a break for it. She's almost free!

Unfortunately, Papa Corn's been lying in wait. He pops up from the shadows, making himself a barrier between Sally and the only way out.

She screams.

Mercilessly, Papa Corn grabs her by the throat and pushes her up against a wall, practically fracturing her windpipe. He slaps her viciously, slams her head into the wall a few more times, and knocks the wind out of her. Finally, he tosses her on the floor like a ragdoll.

"Leave her alone!" quivering Don blubbers from the periphery.

Papa ignores him.

Profoundly injured and crying profusely, Sally tries to pray.

"Please... please God... help me..."

"Think about in who's direction you are looking when you bow your head to pray, bitch," Papa tells her while wiping drool from his chin. "It ain't God's!"

Sally struggles to her feet and tries to run back into the dark theater. But Papa Corn grabs her by the hair and jerks her back so hard she flies off her feet. When she hits the floor this time, she's too broken to struggle.

Papa Corn yanks Don's leash and brings him close.

"Look alive, Donald!" He's growing giddy. "It's the greatest show on Earth! And you've got a front-row seat!" He releases the leash, allowing Don to slump on the floor.

Papa Corns struts back over to Sally like a stray cat, anticipating the coming climax. He throws his jacket on the floor.

"What are you gonna do to her?" Don asks, despite knowing exactly what he's going to do with her.

"I'm gonna do what I do," Papa replies matter-of-factly. "I'm gonna rape her, slit her throat, and give what's left of her to Noodledome to play with... Unless you've got a better suggestion, Donald."

"Just let her go," drained Don groans. "Don't kill her, man. She doesn't deserve to die."

"How do you know?" Papa Corn challenges.

Don looks over at Sally, semiconscious and already bleeding on the floor. She isn't much older than Alyssa.

"I just know," Don sobs, suddenly overcome with the desire to rescue Sally. "Don't hurt her."

Papa Corn's reply is sardonic.

"You *just know*?" he scoffs. "That's cute."

Papa approaches Don and sits down on the floor beside him. He puts his arm around Don's shoulder like they're old chums. He's suddenly furious and punches Don in his eye. It's certain to be a shiner.

"From the first sin of birth, we all deserve to die!" Papa Corn hollers into Don's smarting face. "Did you *just know* your wife was putting Choco in her taco?"

"Fuck you!" Don screams back in a rare (if ineffectual) act of defiance.

"Did you *just know* you were gonna kill people tonight?" Papa belittles.

"Of course not!"

"That's because you don't know shit!" Papa can't stop his fiery tirade; foam flies from his lips as he pontificates. "But do know this, Donald, and don't you ever doubt it; everyone that died tonight, every single fucking one, all died for the very same reason. And do you know what that reason is?" Papa Corn's face is mere inches away from Don's when he says, "Because... I... chose... you."

Floodgates open. Pent-up tears roll down Don's cheeks.

It's true! Don thinks. *It's all my fault!*

Papa Corn turns back to Sally, intending to TCB.

Sally opens her eyes and manages to sit up just as Papa comes back for her. She's never been more afraid.

Papa Corn tosses off his suspenders. His pinstriped trousers drop in a manner that would be comical if it wasn't so disgusting. He reaches down and strokes Little Papa as it grows.

"No!" Sally screams when she sees the little clown's face.

Papa Corn throws his voice down to his dick.

"I get what I want!" it proclaims in a cartoonish voice.

Sally screams for her life as Papa Corn crawls on top of her.

"Mmm..." Papa groans and gurgles. "Screaming only makes it better."

Sally's screams transition into sobs as Papa Corn spreads her legs and gets into position.

"No!" Don howls, switching into beast-mode. He's got some fight left in him yet!

They say a person only knows who they are when their back's against the wall. It took a long fucking time, but Don remembers who he really is. He's a man! And he cannot allow these atrocities to commence a single moment longer!

He springs off the floor and kicks Papa Corn hard enough to dislodge him from Sally's body. He remembers that Papa keeps a gun in his jacket. He moves fast! Don grabs it, cocks it, and points it at his supreme oppressor.

As soon as Papa Corn gets to his feet, Don aims at his heart and shoots.

Time seems to slow down as the bullet makes contact. Don sees the instant Papa Corn registers what just happened. There's an expression of fear; a nanosecond later... pride. Then, as the bullet passes through his body, a smile.

I'm so proud of you, Donald—but Papa doesn't even have time to think about it. He closes his eyes, falls to the floor, and moves no more.

"Fuck you, you sick son of a bitch!" Don's catharsis is unparalleled, but there's no time to pat himself on the back yet. They've got to get the fuck out of there fast.

He attempts to assist a traumatized Sally up from the floor.

"Don't touch me!" she screams, hitting and slapping Don away.

"I'm not one of them," Don assures her, despite his attire and make-up. "I'm not one of those goddamn clowns!"

Sally listens, bewildered.

"They kidnapped me," Don continues. "They took my kids! You're safe now, but we've got to hurry!"

Sally finally feels somewhat comforted. She gets to her feet as Don swiftly locates a cell phone in Papa Corn's satchel.

"Call the police!" Sally begs.

"I will," Don promises. "As soon as I find out where my daughters are, we're getting the fuck outta here."

"Okay, but hurry!" Sally pleads. As Don continues scrolling through text messages, she looks down at Papa Corn's body. His face is splattered with blood. "Is he dead?" she asks.

"Here it is!" Don rejoices. "24th and West County Road!"

"Let's go!" Sally screams, nearly at her wits' end again.

But Don doesn't go just yet. He's got too much rage to display intelligent decision-making capabilities. He just *has* to kick the shit out of Papa Corn's lifeless body. Just for a minute.

"You fucking piece of shit!" Don kicks with vehemence.

"How does it fucking feel when someone *else* plays God? You fucker!"

"Stop it!" Sally breaks the rage-spell and Don returns to his senses. "Come on!"

Don agrees.

They rush the double doors but, to their consternation, they seem to be blocked from outside.

"Fuck!" Don yells. "Let's go back out through the front."

"We can't! The other ones are out there!"

Don thinks.

"Let's find a safe place to hide and call 911."

It was a good plan, Don had. They started to retreat. But it's already too late.

"Oh, Donald..."

Papa Corn rises slowly off the floor.

Sally shrieks.

"You weren't gonna leave without saying goodbye, were you Donald?" Papa Corn sounds sincerely hurt; the truth is, he couldn't be happier. He regards the new hole in his shoulder and looks back at Don. "You shot me. I'm... so... proud!"

"How?" Don replies, mystified.

No, Papa Corn isn't undead or immortal or secretly a vampire. He's just a psycho-sexual sadist with a very high pain threshold. He loves pain.

Also, Don happens to be an incredibly poor marksman.

"You did it all by yourself!" Papa Corn continues praising Don. "You pulled the trigger, fully intending to take a life." His smile widens. "Now you're a killer. Just... like... me!"

"I'm nothing like you!"

"We're like two peas in a pod," Papa Corn insists.

And when Don thinks about everything he's done, he realizes he lacks moral high ground.

"Except for shooting me, you've done everything I asked. You killed people at my behest, and now you're really good at it. And as a reward for how far you've come, I've decided I will indeed let you see your daughters again. Very, very soon."

"Then it's all over?" Don asks.

"Not quite."

Papa Corn blows his whistle, summoning Pepe the Chainsaw Juggling Mime.

Like a wraith, Pepe appears behind Sally. The relative silence is obliterated when he revs his deadly machine back to life. Before Sally can react, the chainsaw rips through her back and out through the front of her torso.

Instinctively, Sally claws at the chainsaw, sending all of her fingers flying.

"No!" Don yells impotently.

Pepe proceeds to chainsaw Sally completely in half. That's two bisections in a single night! Top that Art the Clown!

While Don's distracted, Papa Corn jabs him in the neck with a metal syringe and buries the plunger.

Don fades into a dream state almost immediately, falling limply to the floor. He still hears bits of conversation, like voices underwater, echoing into the purple haze.

"Don't you love a happy ending?"

Outside, Mister Blister and Noodledome unbolt the back exit and enter the loading area. Jumbo's right behind them, having just ditched Deputy Potts' patrol car in a quarry. The Camero can be heard idling close by.

"Let's make it snappy, boys."

Everyone springs into action, erasing the evidence.

Noodledome wraps the two halves of Sally in a plastic tarp like a burrito. Once secured with duct-tape, he throws her over his shoulder and out to the trunk of the Camero. He thinks there's room for just one more!

Pepe the Mime follows. He'll be riding back in the trunk too.

As Jumbo mops up the blood and viscera, Mister Blister grabs drugged-out Don by the collar.

"Do you think he's ready?" Mister Blister asks Papa Corn while blowing a cloud of smoke.

"Oh, he's ready," Papa Corn replies, looking into Don's eyes as he passes out completely. "It's showtime!"

BILL OBERST JR

CIRCUS OF THE DEAD

PAPA CORN THE CLOWN

ELL COW FILMS BLOODY BILL PRODUCTION 'CIRCUS OF THE DEAD' BILL OBERST JR • PARRISH RANDALL • CHANEL RYAN

BILLY PON ROGER EDWARDS RYAN CLAPP RUSTY EDWARDS MIKE WILLIAMS BRAD POTTS TIFFANI FEST JED DUESLER AND SERGIO GRACIDA

ODDTOPSY FX ANTHONY GUTIERREZ LAUREN MORRIS GAEB RAMIREZ PON BING CHUN AARON RAY BALLARD MELISSA LAND BILLY PON & LEE ANKRUM BILLY PON

CircusOfTheDeadMovie.com

RUSTY EDWARDS

MISTER B ER CLOWN

BELL COW FILMS BLOODY BILL PRODUCTION 'CIRCUS OF THE DEAD' BILL OBERST JR • PARRISH RANDALL • CHANEL RYAN

BILLY PON ROGER EDWARDS RYAN CLAPP RUSTY EDWARDS MIKE WILLIAMS BRAD POTTS TIFFANI FEST JED DUESLER AND SERGIO GRACIDA

ODDTOPSY FX ANTHONY GUTIERREZ LAUREN MORRIS GAEB RAMIREZ PON BING CHUN AARON RAY BALLARD MELISSA LAND BILLY PON & LEE ANKRUM BILLY PON

CircusOfTheDeadMovie.com

RYAN CLAPP

NOODLEDOME THE CLOWN

LL COW FILMS PRESENTS A BLOODY BILL PRODUCTION 'CIRCUS OF THE DEAD' BILL OBERST JR • PARRISH RANDALL • CHANEL RYAN

BILLY PON ROGER EDWARDS RYAN CLAPP RUSTY EDWARDS MIKE WILLIAMS BRAD POTTS TIFFANI FEST JED DUESLER AND SERGIO GRACIDA AS BULL BOY

ODTOPSY FX ANTHONY GUTIERREZ LAUREN MORRIS GAED RAMIREZ PON BING CHUN AARON RAY BALLARD MELISSA LAND BILLY PON & LEE ANKRUM BILLY PON

CircusOfTheDeadMovie.com

MIKE WILLIAMS
JUMBO THE CLOWN
LL COW FILMS BLOODY BILL PRODUCTION 'CIRCUS OF THE DEAD' BILL OBERST JR • PARRISH RANDALL • CHANEL RYAN
BILLY PON
ROGER EDWARDS RYAN CLAPP RUSTY EDWARDS MIKE WILLIAMS BRAD POTTS TIFFANI FEST JED DUESLER AND SERGIO GRACIDA
ODDTOPSY FX ANTHONY GUTIERREZ LAUREN MORRIS GAEB RAMIREZ PON BING CHUN AARON RAY BALLARD MELISSA LAND BILLY PON & LEE ANKRUM BILLY PON
CircusOfTheDeadMovie.com

PARRISH RANDALL
CIRCUS OF THE DEAD
DONALD THE CLOWN
BELL COW FILMS BLOODY BILL PRODUCTION 'CIRCUS OF THE DEAD' BILL OBERST JR • PARRISH RANDALL • CHANEL RYAN
BILLY PON
ROGER EDWARDS RYAN CLAPP RUSTY EDWARDS MIKE WILLIAMS BRAD POTTS TIFFANI FEST JED DUESLER AND SERGIO GRACIDA
ODDTOPSY FX ANTHONY GUTIERREZ LAUREN MORRIS GAEB RAMIREZ PON BING CHUN AARON RAY GALLARDO MELISSA LAND BILLY PON LEE ANKRUM BILLY PON
CircusOfTheDeadMovie.com

KYLE MUELLER
DEAD
PEPE THE CHAINSAW JUGGLING MIME
LL COW FILMS BLOODY BILL PRODUCTION 'CIRCUS OF THE DEAD' BILL OBERST JR • PARRISH RANDALL • CHANEL RYAN
BILLY PON
ROGER EDWARDS RYAN CLAPP RUSTY EDWARDS MIKE WILLIAMS BRAD POTTS TIFFANI FEST JED DUESLER SERGIO GRACIDA
ODDTOPSY FX ANTHONY GUTIERREZ LAUREN MORRIS GAED RAMIREZ PON BING CHUN AARON RAY BALLARD MELISSA LAND BILLY PON & LEE ANKRUM BILLY PON
CircusOfTheDeadMovie.com

SERGIO GRACIDA
DEAD
DOLL BOY
BLOODY BILL PRODUCTION 'CIRCUS OF THE DEAD' BILL OBERST JR · PARRISH RANDALL · CHANEL RYAN
BILLY PON
ROGER EDWARDS RYAN CLAPP RUSTY EDWARDS MIKE WILLIAMS BRAD POTTS TIFFANI FEST JED DUESLER SERGIO GRACIDA
ANTHONY GUTIERREZ LAUREN MORRIS GAEB RAMIREZ PON BING CHUN AARON RAY BALLARD MELISSA LAND BILLY PON LEE ANKRUM BILLY PON
CircusOfTheDeadMovie.com

CHAPTER 27

UN ÚLTIMO ESPECTÁCULO (ONE LAST SHOW)

"Rise and shine, Donald."

Don Johnson's hellish night is over, but he's still in Hell. He opens his eyes to find himself in a storage closet.

How long have I been unconscious? He wonders as his eyes adjust to the light. Around him, several women are gagged with their arms chained to the ceiling. They're all dead.

Papa Corn's dressed in his Keystone Kops outfit. He yanks Don out by the collar, manhandling him before throwing him into the makeup/torture chair.

Don manages to get a look at Jumbo and the little girl in the Easter dress sitting on the couch, watching a Mexican talk show on TV. The little boy with the balloons on his wrists is still sitting beside the girl, but Don can see he's clearly dead.

The goldfish are dead too, floating belly-up in their murky bowl. Rest in Peace.

Mister Blister, also in his Kop costume, straps Don down.

Don sees a plethora of recently severed heads scattered about the room. It's like they're all staring at him angrily, accusatorially.

Papa Corn takes a seat directly across from Don.

"It's your big day, Donald," he says. "I've got a big surprise for you."

Papa Corn reaches into his pocket and pulls out a cell phone. He scrolls through the videos, presses PLAY, and turns the screen around for Don to see.

Alyssa and Hillary are tied to the same chairs in the same nondescript, dirty building. They probably haven't moved in days and certainly look worse for the wear. It's another statement made under extreme duress.

"Read!" Mister Blister barks from behind the camera.

Jumbo, cue cards in hand, yips.

"H-hi, Dad," Alyssa croaks. "Papa says this is our last video. H-he says you'll be seeing us real soon." She seems hopeless, despite the encouraging words she just recited.

Don's immediately overwhelmed and starts weeping.

"W-we love you and we miss you," Alyssa finishes as Jumbo charges them with the cattle prod, cackling like an evil imp.

The video ends with Don's daughters screaming, descending once again into a state of traumatic delirium.

Don closes his tear-filled eyes as Papa Corn puts the cellphone back in his pocket.

There's a jolting knock at the door.

"Clowns, five minutes. Five minutes, clowns!" a voice outside shouts.

"Come now, Donald," Papa Corn consoles. "It's almost over. Now let's go finish what we've started."

Papa Corn wraps duct-tape around Don's mouth and paints a red smile over his lips.

"Showtime!"

Mister Blister unstraps Don as the entire crew lines up by the door.

At the other end of Clown Alley, inside the Big Top, the Ringmaster is whipping the crowd into a rambunctious frenzy.

"Who do you want?" she asks the crowd, pumping her arms up and down.

"We want the clowns!"

"I can't hear you!"

"We want the clowns!"

"Keep it going!"

The crowd stomps and chants as they raise their voices even higher.

"We want the clowns! We want the clowns! We want the clowns..."

"Never let anyone say that Circo Gigante doesn't give the people what they want!"

The cheers and applause are booming.

"You wanted 'em! Now you're gonna get 'em! Send in the clowns!"

The clowns roll in on their Model-T, much to the crowd's elation.

Papa Corn steps out beneath the spotlight.

"Ladies and Gentlemen," he yells in his exaggerated clown voice through his huge fake mustache. "There is a prisoner among you!"

A spotlight hits the bleachers, illuminating Jumbo as he drags the shackled Don out of the audience. As he gets closer, Noodledome and Mister Blister grab the prisoner by the arms and toss him back into the ring like wrestlers. The crowd loves the theatrics.

"Shall we do justice?" Papa Corn asks the audience.

The crowd replies in the affirmative.

Mister Blister, Noodledome, and Jumbo surround Don, kicking him and beating him with their weapons of choice.

Don clenches up and takes the abuse. He glances out at the unhinged audience; they're loving every second of it. His eyes linger on a family in the stand, sitting almost exactly where he and his family sat just a few days ago.

Don hopes the father is thankful for what he's got. At that moment, he'd do anything to trade places with him. And isn't *that* what Papa Corn's been trying to teach him this entire time?

Don starts to laugh through his muzzle, even though he's being whacked with a mallet, cracked with a bat, and struck with a pipe. He finally sees the light.

Thank you, Papa Corn!

His wife may be dead, but he still has his daughters. Eventually, he'll meet someone new. No one can ever replace Tiffany, but the kids will have another mother. They'll be happy and Don will never take the beauty of life for granted again.

The cops will believe me, he thinks, *especially with modern DNA improvements and crime solving techniques... Right?*

Sure, he'll do some jail time, but his daughters will be safe and, eventually, they'll all be back together. They're all that really matters.

"Shall we use the prod?" Papa Corn asks the bloodthirsty audience.

They begin chanting immediately.

"Prod! Prod! Prod..."

"They say yes!"

Papa Corn blasts Don with the sizzling cattle-prod.

As he convulses uncontrollably, teeth chattering, Don wonders for the first time, *What ever happened to Brandon?*

The assault concludes, leaving Don a bloody mess in the dirt.

"Thank you, Ladies and Gentlemen, for ensuring justice... reigns... in... America!"

The clowns get a standing ovation, and they bow to thank the cheering spectators.

Papa Corn leans down for an intimate conversation with Don. He pulls the duct-tape off the prisoner's mouth.

"Congratulations Donald. It's all over. You won."

"Thank you, Papa!" Don replies as tears of relief flow down his face. "I'm sorry I didn't appreciate my family..."

"Donald, you are most definitely welcome..." Papa smiles, becoming tender. "I'm going to miss you, Donald. This is the end of the road for us, I'm afraid. It's time for you and I to say adios and happy trails."

Don looks confused as Papa Corn sticks a metal syringe into his neck and buries the plunger. He immediately starts floating, his eyelids heavy, the crowds' din diminishing into white noise.

"This is the last time you will ever see me. When you wake up, you will see your daughters."

"You promise me?"

Papa Corn grins sweetly. His piercing blue eyes seem authentically kind. His voice is barely a whisper.

"Yes, I promise. Sweet dreams, Donald."

Don manages a half-smile before he passes out.

CHAPTER 28

VÓMITO (PUKE)

There's a TV set playing in the corner of the morgue.

News 7 cuts in with breaking news.

"The death toll rises to thirteen," Angela Maverick informs her viewers. "Police are still unable to locate prime suspect Donald Arthur Johnson..."

The same unflattering photo of dipshit Don fills the screen.

"...or his daughters, fourteen-year-old Alyssa Johnson and ten-year-old Hillary Johnson. This man is considered armed and extremely dangerous. If you see him, do not try to apprehend him on your own. Please call 911 immediately if..."

No one in the room's paying attention. Three men are leaning over a metal gurney, leering at Tiffany Johnson's naked, headless body.

"Gentlemen," Steve the coroner says to Detective Roper

and Officer Goodson. "I can state conclusively that this body's been gnawed on by something... and it wasn't an animal!"

"What was it, Doc?" Officer Goodson asks, unable to peel his eyes away from what remains of Tiffany.

"If I didn't know better, I'd say we're dealing with a pack of cannibals!"

No one says anything. No one turns away from the spectacle of Tiffany's body.

"I'll tell you what, Detective," Steve continues, "Don Johnson's one sick son of a bitch!"

"Yes, he is," Detective Roper concurs. "But you know we're gonna get him, right?"

"Oh yeah, I know," Steve confidently replies. "I just wonder how many more people are gonna die before you do?"

"I still can't believe one man did all of this," Roper says, shaking his head.

Steve takes off his latex gloves.

"What are we gonna do about T.C. and Mrs. Johnson's affair?" he asks.

Detective Roper raises his cowboy hat above his brow and gazes around the morgue before he replies.

"Nothing," he says emphatically. "We're gonna keep it between us."

Steve nods his head and sighs.

Queasy Officer Deacon bursts loudly through the doors, scaring the shit out of everyone.

"Je-sus!" Roper replies angrily. "What is it, Deacon?"

Officer Deacon opens his mouth to speak but catches a glimpse of Tiffany's body behind them. Instead, he pukes all over the floor.

Everyone cringes.

"Not again!" Roper's getting frustrated. "You got more vomitus than any cop I've ever met!"

"I'm sorry," Officer Deacon apologizes, wiping drizzle off his chin.

"Well, spit it out!"

"We've located Don Johnson, sirs!" Deacon says.

"Where?" Roper asks.

"Music City Mall."

"Well, what are we waiting for? Let's go!"

Steve watches Detective Roper and Officer Rose sprint out, avoiding the vomit on the floor.

"Godspeed, Gentlemen."

CHAPTER 29

EL MUÑECO (THE DOLL)

"Hey! Wake up!"

After tying up a few loose ends, Papa Corn and his core crew have reconvened in a dilapidated doghouse on the edge of the oilfield.

"Now, I know what you're thinking," Papa continues as Mister Blister, Noodledome, and Jumbo look on. "I said it was time for you and I to go our separate ways and that you'd never see me again. Well, guess what? I lied."

The other clowns have a good chuckle, imagining his shocked surprise and crushing disappointment.

"I said, wake up!" Papa Corn yells, straddling Brandon and slapping him in the face until he opens his eyes. "There you are!" Papa pops off his lap.

Brandon's groggy and confused. The duct-tape's been removed from around his mouth, but his lips are still stapled shut. He assesses the situation and gets real scared real fast.

"Good morning, sunshine," Papa Corn sweetly croons.

Brandon sits before a huge industrial-size refrigeration unit—wrapped in chains. He's been in this situation before. He already knows what's inside.

Brandon moans.

Papa Corn smiles, Mister Blister smokes, Noodledome munches chips, and Jumbo plays with his chihuahua puppet.

"I know I said you were well on the way to achieving self-actualization..." Papa Corn circles the box, keeping his eyes on Brandon. "But circumstances have changed."

Brandon struggles, but it's no use. He isn't going anywhere.

"Unfortunately, we've raised our standards and decided, as a group," he motions around to the others, "that you just don't quite measure up." Papa holds his fingers three inches apart.

Brandon tries to yell through his stapled lips, causing his cheeks to puff out and sending snot streaming down his nose.

"Nevertheless," Papa Corn continues. "We'd like to thank you for your valiant efforts and wish you luck in your... future endeavors."

More chuckling from the peanut gallery.

Mister Blister lights a fresh cigarette.

"Are you even listening to me, asshole?" Papa Corn scolds Brandon for his lack of manners. "Yes? No? Oh, well. You'll figure it out soon enough. Happy trails to you, Brandon! Till we meet again, shithead! Have fun with The Babysitter!"

Brandon weeps. *Not again!*

"Mister Noodledome, if you would be so kind."

As Mister Blister and Jumbo gather their gear and head out, Papa and Noodledome proceed to the box.

Noodledome opens a series of rusty locks until all the chains loosen and fall to the floor.

The box is silent.

Papa Corn picks up an old tin can on a string that runs from the refrigerator and speaks.

"I brought you something," he whispers into the can. "A gift... the one who got away..."

Something inside the box begins to stir.

"Finish what you started..." Papa continues, "and you will be one of us. Papa loves you." He kisses the box before turning back to Noodledome. "Did you secure the bait in the van?"

Noodledome smiles and nods.

"Well then," Papa replies, "let's make like a tree and get the fuck outta here."

Papa Corn and Noodledome walk away, leaving Brandon alone.

Brandon strains against the bailing wire that binds him again; but, as always, they just won't budge! He hears something big stirring in the icebox, as though emerging from a deep slumber. To his escalating horror, the door slowly opens to reveal... Doll Boy!

Yes, the ominous Babysitter and the infamous Doll Boy are one and the same! Two personas coalescing into one. The metamorphosis is almost complete.

He emerges from the box like an outcast Nephilim: a mountain of a man dressed like a child; his face, hidden by a sinister, cracked baby mask! He's dragging a massive hammer!

Brandon screams ineffectually as Doll Boy lumbers toward him, raising his unholy hammer. It's a moment the beast has been pinning for—a second chance to kill the one who go away. Time to complete the circle.

Doll Boy swings, landing a direct blow to Brandon's chest, knocking him over.

Brandon struggles for breath. His ribs have been shattered and his organs are bleeding internally. On his back, coughing and gagging, Brandon's eyes widen as Doll Boy comes in for the kill.

Doll Boy raises the sledgehammer over his head and brings it down in a powerful arc, crushing Brandon's head.

Brandon practically welcomes death. Adios, Asshole.

The caterpillar is now a butterfly.

CHAPTER 30

LA MUERTE (THE DEATH)

Don wakes up in the parking lot of a shopping mall, outside a food court. It's early dawn, but the sky still retains a hint of nighttime. The Sun's about to peek over the horizon as a street sweeper passes by.

Slowly, he realizes that he's sitting in his own car, dressed in his own clothes. His clown make-up has been crudely wiped off and his wounds haphazardly bandaged. He sighs deeply, thinking it's all over. Then he looks down at his hands.

Weary and confused, he tries to clear the cobwebs out of his head.

He's holding Jumbo's snub-nosed .357—but why?

He finds the answer in his other hand—but he doesn't like it. Not one bit.

He's holding a couple of Loteria cards, the last two from Papa Corn's deck. On top, Los Ninos—The Children. It's been

X-ed out with a black marker. Below that: La Muerte—The Death. Clean with no X. His heart sinks when he puts the pieces together.

"No..."

He looks at the gun, then back at the cards, and then back to the gun again.

"No..."

His eyes fill with dread. He senses something bad has happened. He slowly, hesitantly gazes up at the rearview mirror.

"NO!"

Don's primal howls fill the parking lot, resonating against nearby buildings and sending flocks of sleeping crows flying.

Alyssa and Hillary are slumped over in the back seat. Their eyes are closed, and their heads are touching one another. Each of Don's daughters has a bullet hole in her forehead.

Another impossibly wounded scream reaches the valleys and vast wastelands.

Don collapses onto the steering wheel, sobbing, inconsolable. He doesn't even notice all the police cars creeping in around him.

"Donald Johnson!" Detective Roper's amplified voice comes from a bullhorn. "This is the police! We have you surrounded! Throw your keys out the window, step out of your vehicle, and face away!"

Let them come and get me, Don thinks, refusing to even lift his head in acknowledgment.

Then he hears an all too familiar voice.

"Don-ald..."

Don slowly raises his head from the steering wheel. Tears are streaming down his face.

In the rearview mirror, Don sees Papa Corn sitting in between his daughters. Their heads are on his shoulders, like peaceful sleeping angels.

Don's eyes fill with hate.

"Fuck you!" Don screams. "Fuck you, you fucking liar!"

"I promised you'd see your daughters again, Donald. And well... here they are."

In the rearview mirror, Don sees Papa Corn holding hands with his daughters. He collapses back onto the steering wheel, sobbing and screaming.

"Donald Johnson!" The bullhorn sounds even louder this time. "This is the police! We have you surrounded! Throw your keys out the window, step out of your vehicle, and face away!"

Detective Roper's just itching to take Don down. Dozens of officers are at the ready, weapons drawn.

"You never knew just how much you loved your family until you lost them." Papa Corns speaks the truth. "And what a shame it is that it took all of this just to realize how happy you actually *were*."

Don wishes he could deny it, but he can't. He brought everything on himself. He's got no one else to blame.

He remembers a recent morning with his family.

"Without you three, I'd be lost." Don's own words echo in his ears. "I'd be nothing. I wouldn't want to be alive if I didn't have you and the girls."

Don knows now that the unmarked Death card is for him. It's the final piece of Papa Corn's demented puzzle. It all comes down to this.

Don takes one last look into the rearview mirror. Papa Corn's gone. His dead daughters remain.

He's about to join them.

Detective Roper's about to yell into his bullhorn for the third time when he hears a single gunshot fired from inside Don Johnson's car.

"Move in!" he orders.

A dozen cops rush forward.

CHAPTER 31

EL MAYOR ESPECTÁCULO DEL MUNDO (THE GREATEST SHOW ON EARTH)

An antique phonograph spins an old record.

Bing Crosby sings "Beautiful Dreamer" accompanied by John Scott Trotter and his orchestra.

There's a knock at the door.

"Clowns, ten minutes! Ten minutes, clowns!"

As his crew files out the front door of the trailer, Papa Corn stays back. He regards the Loteria card sheets taped to the walls. So many beautiful X's! He lingers on La Muerte—The Death card, the final one crossed off.

"Happy trails, Donald," he whispers.

A moment later, Papa Corns pulls down the marked-up Loteria sheets, tearing them to shreds and crumpling them into balls.

Beneath the yellow light of a lamp Noodledome constructed from the body of the balloon boy, Papa covers the walls with brand-new unmarked Loteria sheets.

The convoy will be packing up soon and heading out to a new city—and a new game will begin.

What, you didn't think that Papa Corn was going to stop killing now that he's completed his mission, did you? Oh, no, no.

And if you thought this was Papa Corn's first Loteria-themed massacre, well, you'd be wrong about that too.

Before joining his cohorts for their final performance in Odessa, Texas, Papa Corn pauses to regard his own reflection in his stained, broken mirror.

"Papa, Papa, Papa..." He smiles, "Papa Corn! Papa Corn! I'm Papa Corn!"

He can already hear the Ringmaster working the crowd into a frenzy.

"Welcome to the greatest show on Earth!"

"We want the clowns! We want the clowns! We want the clowns..."

Soon, the circus may be coming to a town near you. Keep your eyes open and your ears peeled.

And before you go, he just wants you to know: "Papa loves you. Papa will always love you."

PREQUEL

WHEN PAPA MET DOLL BOY (A LOVE STORY)

CHAPTER 1

EL VENDEDOR DE HELADO (THE ICE-CREAM MAN)

"Ice-cream man, ice-cream man, what do you see?" Papa Corn whispers. "I see hairless puppies looking at me..."

He's behind the wheel of the beat-up circus van; Noodledome's sitting shotgun, holding a sawed-off shotgun. Mister Blister, Jumbo, and a dying prostitute are playing Russian Roulette in the back.

"That *hombre* right there," Papa tells Noodledome, "is a special kind of sicko... I think I want to be his friend."

He points at a rundown, unsanitary blue & white ice-cream truck idling in front of an expansive block of apartments. It's surrounded by clamoring children who don't seem to notice (or care) that the truck's coated in mildew and belching blue smoke that stinks.

Leaning out the window, an obese balding man in a filthy apron passes out Push-Ups, Bomb-Pops, Big Dippers and dripping cones as fast as he can.

"Bringing joy to both kinds... girls and boys with treats both sweet and sticky..." Papa Corn begins to drool. "Behind his smile he doth beguile, for his mind is vile and tricky!"

Noodledome smiles and nods his head; he's also beginning to drool.

"You know what they say," Papa continues. "Birds of a feather fuck together!"

Papa and Noodledome share a hearty laugh; shy Noodledome covers his smile with his hand. Their jovial expressions are interrupted, however, when a gunshot rings out from the back. BANG! After a pregnant pause, the silence is broken by the sound of Jumbo yipping like a dog.

He hikes up his leg and urinates on the dead prostitute.

Mister Blister lights a fresh cigarette to mask the odor of spent gunpowder.

"She's all yours, Noodledome," the pyromaniac announces, wiping the hookers' blood and brains off of his jacket.

Papa Corn rolls his eyes and shakes his head.

"Mister Noodledome," Papa says, "please remind me to talk to Mister Blister about what I mean when I say 'inconspicuous.'"

Noodledome nods as he and Papa Corn turn their attention back to the ice-cream truck and its corpulent attendant.

Mister Blister and Jumbo creep forward from the back of the van to have a look-see for themselves.

"FREE ICE CREAM" is painted in sloppy block letters on both sides of the truck (with small print reading, *"One ice cream per child under 14"*).

"What are you thinking, boss?" Mister Blister asks, blowing a cloud of smoke. "Blast the lard-ass and nab the sperm-letts?"

"No..." Papa Corn replies. "While that would certainly be a

satisfying way to spend the afternoon, I find that idea somewhat... short-sighted." He's captivated by the ice-cream man. "I spy a degenerate of unusual potential. A kindred cousin..."

As though sensing eight evil eyes upon him, Hugo Gutiérrez looks across a sea of children's heads, spotting the beat-up van parked down the street. For a moment, everyone freezes.

Are those clowns looking at me? The ice-cream man wonders, his jaw tightening.

"Gimme ice cream!" Little Juanito demands, bringing Hugo's attention back to his boisterous customers.

The ice-cream man smiles, passing a soggy pink cone out the window with his left hand while rubbing his crotch with his right.

"Here you go, machito. It's today's Super-Secret-Special Flavor. I made it myself last night!"

"Gracias, heladero!" Little Juanito says, taking a huge bite and scurrying off.

"No, thank *you*," Hugo mutters under his breath. "I think I'll be seeing you later!"

Today's Super-Secret-Special Flavor, by the way, is Flesh 'n' Fentanyl.

When he looks back across the street, the beat-up van and its grease-painted occupants are nowhere to be seen. Maybe he imagined them. PCP is a helluva drug.

* * *

For a week now, The Big Old Circus has been grounded in Brownsville, Texas owing to a perfect storm of cluster-fucks.

Thanks to a politician in DC getting folks riled-up over immigration, Tia Colibrí, the esteemed aerial artist, was stuck in Matamoros after dipping below the border to visit family.

Two elephants had died recently after someone (definitely not Mister Blister) fed them each a pound of Floridian meth. The Big Top tent got ripped up in a cyclone. The company doctor died from auto-erotic asphyxiation, and the Lady Ringmaster went on the run with a coven of bitches. (Yes, bitches.)

Everything would work itself out in time. Tia Colibrí would find her way back and a couple of new elephants were en route to the Bluewing Royal Terminal in the Port of Brownsville via Honduras. You can get anything and everything you need on the border of Mexico — and it's usually cheap! Tents would be mended, vacant positions would be filled, and the Lady Ringmaster would return home—eventually.

But a stationary existence is inopportune for murderous sadists of the nomadic variety, like Papa Corn and his posse. Sprees were out of the question, as even the Keystone Kops can follow blood-trails back to a rooted perpetrator. Every random act of violence had to be weighed on a scale that balanced pleasure with consequences.

It was downright annoying, especially for Mister Blister, who could be the most head-strong of the bunch. He also had an independent streak that saw him straining for composure when Papa kept him confined to the Clown Trailer at night. The potential for clown-on-clown violence was escalating.

Instead of releasing their profane urges in blasts of blissful chaos, Papa Corn and his crew spent time on "special projects" that were easier to keep on the down low—like new recruits. They were random victims (unwilling pledges) from various stops, stuffed into the corners of their mobile house of horrors. Losers and castaways that no one will miss, the dregs of humanity who Papa Corn hopes to reeducate—or maybe even share a connection with.

They usually die. Some will end up in Mama Gordo's

Freak Show Menagerie, strung out on meth or another drug of choice. (Hell, Lil' Lou Lou's drug of choice is fried chicken. She eats a lot of it. Her diabetes is gonna kill her quicker than meth, I promise!)

But every once in a while, someone emerges from Papa's program completely refreshed, rehabilitated, and reborn. A true collaborator.

Like Pepe, the Chainsaw Juggling Mime, for example. Once a lowlife peeping-tom with a Benadryl addiction, he'd earned his way into the show. That motherfucker can juggle anything; he once juggled two and a half newborns. What a sight! Papa found it much easier to mentor the motor-mouth after removing his bottom jaw.

Now, Pepe, the Chainsaw Juggling Mime, roams the corridors of the Clown Trailer unbound, sporting what looks like a perpetual Columbian necktie. He remains on-alert, waiting to be summoned by Papa's shrill rape whistle.

Everyone's united in promoting Pepe's future success. Papa Corn helps him hone his persona, Jumbo sews him a stylish outfit, Mister Blister teaches him chainsaw mechanics, and Noodledome tinkers on a new prosthetic jaw. Pepe's part of the family now, or at least a first cousin of sorts.

But Papa's always thinking about the future and, tonight, he's thinking about that ice-cream man.

* * *

After a productive day of drugging and mistreating children, Hugo drives back to his dilapidated trailer on the edge of the Gulf Coast Planes. The sun's gone down by the time he pulls his truck behind a pile of rusty junk that's almost twenty feet high. Even though he doesn't have any neighbors, Hugo covers his truck with a gigantic blue tarp before heading inside his trailer.

He doesn't realize that, this time, he's been followed home.

Inside, Hugo puts a beat-up copy of *Sweatin' to the Oldies* in the VCR before plopping down on his beat-up faux-leather recliner. His plan is to get high on a couple of laced joints and an entire pack of Mexican Viagra before grabbing a shower. If he's still conscious when the sun comes up, he'll eat another pack of fake Viagra before mixing up the day's Super-Secret-Special Flavor (Head Cheese 'n' Methadone).

Outside, the clowns stash their van behind some bushes before beginning their initial reconnaissance. Like ninjas, they quietly make their way towards the ice-cream truck, keen to see what horrors lay within.

Jumbo's giddy.

"Mister Blister, Noodledome," Papa says. "Would you two be so kind as to lift this tarp?"

The tall clowns comply.

With the back of the ice-cream truck accessible, Papa Corn grabs both handles of the rusted double doors.

"Now," he says, "Let's see what this sick fuck's really been up to!"

Papa Corn swings the back doors open with a flourish. A humid mist escapes into the hot nighttime air. Soon enough, the truck's ungodly cargo is revealed.

"Just as I thought!"

Mister Blister, Noodledome, and Jumbo lean in to have a look. You might not know it just by looking at their faces, but each one of them is sufficiently impressed.

"So much beautiful crimson and clover..." Papa Corn whispers. "The ice-cream man's cups do truly runneth over..."

There are at least a dozen kids stuffed in the back of the truck. Half of them are dead, but all of them are practically cocooned in duct-tape. Those who can still move squirm and heave desperately. The ones who aren't blindfolded regard the quartet of curious clowns with pleading eyes, praying for salvation.

"¡Dios mío!" Jumbo yips. "¡No ves eso todos los días!"

Mister Blister casually flicks his lit cigarette butt at the kids, pulls a freshy out from behind his ear, and puts it in his mouth.

"We should call this guy next time we need a babysitter," he says while flipping his Zippo.

"No more playing on the slide or teeter-totter," Papa Corn whispers. "Wrapped up like veal—young lambs to the slaughter..." He sighs. "I told you this demented fuck was something special." Papa slams the back doors closed on the traumatized children and turns to face his troops.

"What now?" Mister Blister asks while blowing a cloud of smoke.

"Now..." Papa Corn's smile turns sinister. "I think it's time for formal introductions."

Noodledome laughs maniacally.

Inside the dank, cum-funky trailer, Hugo's already high as a motherfucker—completely out of his mind on PCP and Mexican brick-weed. His pants are around his ankles, allowing his semi-erection to bob up and down, dancing to the beat with Richard Simmons on TV. His eyes are bloodshot, his pupils completely dilated.

The degenerate pedo's losing his grip on reality. The walls and furniture inside Hugo's trailer melt and morph. Before long, he thinks he's been transported into a Max Fleischer cartoon: two-dimensional, black & white, and nightmarish.

BANG! An impossibly large shoe on an impossibly long leg kicks the door down.

Hugo's instantly frozen in place.

Four cartoon clowns enter single file, dancing a spastic jitterbug.

Hugo's face explodes with delight.

"Is the circus in town?" Hugo *thinks* he asks (when in actuality he's spewing indecipherable gibberish). "Come on in, amigos. Let's party!" God damn, he's never tripped *this* hard before!

He's a cartoon character now too, but the animation style has switched from Fleischer to *Yellow Submarine*, bright and psychedelic. As the four freaky clowns creep closer, Hugo's bloated stomach grows an upside-down face that smiles; his dick becomes a purple snake that slithers under the sofa.

Hugo gurgles towards his unexpected guests.

"Whoa," he marvels. "Are you guys seeing this?"

Suddenly, the clown who most resembles Steamboat Willy jumps into Hugo's lap.

"The ice-cream man stirs his creamy nuts," the clown whispers, "with arms and legs so mangled... But he'll be sorry when he wakes and finds himself entangled!"

The animation style switches to *Looney Tunes* as the tuxedo-wearing clown pulls an impossibly large metal syringe from inside his jacket pocket.

Hugo's eyes pop off his face in enlarging triplicate.

"What the hell's going on here?" he blubbers, alarmed, but still inebriated beyond any defensive capability.

The animation style switches to *The Simpsons*.

"I do apologize, mighty Polyphemus," the clown replies, burying the menacing needle into Hugo's neck. "But we're mere mortals, and therefore no match for the terror you can most certainly inflict." The clown injects his poison. "We'll talk more... when you awaken... Sweet dreams..."

Hugo's fat mouth falls open. His fat tongue falls out, dripping milky saliva. The despicable knuckle-dragger fades into warm oblivion.

* * *

Hugo dreams of being a baby again, biting off his mother's nipples. He dreams he's the King of Ice-Cream Land, living in a milk chocolate castle dripping with cherries and melted marshmallows. He dreams of throbbing rockets blasting into clenched black holes. Beautiful, wonderful, precious dreams... until he's snapped back into reality by an icy blast.

Mister Blister dumps a bucket of piss and ice-water over the ice-cream man's head. The disgusting lump wakes with a start, finding himself face-to-face with four very real, very sadistic circus clowns.

"Rise and shine, asshole," Mister Blister says.

Noodledome's laughing hysterically.

Jumbo's yipping and yapping.

Papa Corn just stares, his pale blue eyes penetrating the ice-cream-man's twisted soul.

"What the fuck's going on here?" Hugo wants to ask, but his mouth is stuffed with something clammy (Noodledome's scabies-infested skivvies), secured with barbed-wire. He's been bound to his recliner with a combination of duct-tape, ropes, and chains.

"I must say," Papa Corn begins in his soothing, hypnotic tone, "You're even more impressive than I imagined. I mean that in the worst possible way. It's wonderful."

Hugo's experiencing sensory overload. It's a lot to take in all at once. Eventually, he looks down at his crotch and gasps. The clowns have been playing..

There's a cinder block between his legs, half of it's buried betwixt Hugo's hairy butt-cheeks, up against his taint. The other half of the cinder block extends forwards. On top of the block, Hugo's dick and balls are splayed prominently.

The head of his circumcised penis has been painted up in clown-face.

Descending into dismay, Hugo struggles and strains, sweats and tries to scream—but it's no use. He isn't going anywhere. He's at the mercy of the clowns.

Papa Corn leans in close until they're almost nose-to-nose.

"When I look at you," he coos, "I see so much... squandered potential."

Hugo's confused.

"So much horror in your heart," Papa strokes the ice-cream man's face tenderly. "So much glorious agony to dispense." His voice turns from happy to disappointed. "Yet you waste the majority of your talents on... disgusting adolescents."

Looking on with his arms crossed, Mister Blister shakes his head, amplifying Papa Corn's disapproval.

"I've no qualms with infanticide, filicide, or sororicide," Papa continues. "But it's just too easy, isn't it? Like killing fish in a barrel." Papa slaps the ice-cream man across his ugly face. "Now, I'm not saying you *shouldn't* murder children. By all means, murder children! But when was the last time you were truly... challenged?"

Papa's voice transitions from disappointed to angry. "When's the last time you went toe-to-toe with someone your own size—or at least over four feet tall? When's the last time you erased an entire pack of able-bodied men and women?" Papa screams, saliva spraying across the ice-cream man's face. "Obsessed with your throbbing nuggets, gorged on low-hanging fruit to the detriment of your untapped greatness!" He grits his teeth. "You make me want to vomit! I should have

Mister Blister cover the walls of this God-awful hovel with your brains!"

Mister Blister pulls his gun from his belt, cocks it, and presses it up against the ice-cream man's left temple.

Hugo's trembling.

"Luckily for you," Papa Corn tells the ice-cream man while signaling for Mister Blister to put his gun away, "I'm a clown with a vision." His voice is soft and soothing again. "I see you for who you will become. Beneath your layers of filth and cellulite, beneath the insipid blob, there's a primal animal about to awaken."

Hugo begins to calm down, believing he might actually survive this encounter. But his relief is short-lived.

"But first..." Papa Corn smiles before shouting in his over-the-top clown voice. "Doctor Noodledome! It's time for a castration! Stat!"

Papa Corn steps aside, allowing shit-grinning Noodledome to step forward. The happy simpleton moves in with a sledgehammer perched on his shoulder; he regards the ice-cream man's face, then looks down at the pervert's disgusting junk.

For Hugo, it's pure, unadulterated panic. He wishes he could retract his testicles and urethra inside his body.

"Trust me," Papa Corn says without a trace of irony, "you'll be much less distracted once we crack your walnuts!"

That's Noodledome's signal to bring down the hammer. It only takes one mighty swing to pulverize the ice-cream man's testicles while irreparably fracturing his shaft. Blood, cum, and pieces of broken cinder block are everywhere. What remains of the ice-cream man's member resembles a mutilated baby armadillo.

Gagged Hugo wants to scream, but he can't. A pain unlike anything he's felt surges through his body like lightning. His eyes feel like they might explode out of his skull. Thankfully, he's able to somersault back into the comparative relief of nightmarish unconsciousness.

"Doctor Noodledome, please attend to our new recruit's injuries while he's sleeping," Papa Corn instructs.

Noodledome pulls a pack of *Sesame Street* Band-Aids from his rusty *Kung-Fu* lunchbox and gets to work reassembling the dangling chunks.

Jumbo sets about ransacking the place.

Mister Blister lights a fresh cigarette.

"You really think he's Big Top material?" Blister asks Papa Corn.

"Almost certain," Papa Corn replies. "At the very least, we can put him to work in Mama Gordo's Freak Show Menagerie!"

"What's next?"

"Next, Mister Blister..." Papa Corn gets a far-away look in his eyes, "we see just how low the ice-cream man can go!"

CHAPTER 2
LA MASSACRE
(THE MASSACRE)

Super Java's the hippest coffeehouse in all of downtown Brownsville. The shameless Starbucks knock-off specializes in hot caffeinated beverages, overloaded with corn syrup, and topped with foam and caramel. Their Venti Frosty Blue Pegasus Double-Shot Oak Latte will set you back upwards of ten bucks.

Sixty-year-old Theodore Newton's the manager. He hates that he hasn't amounted to more in life. He wears a collared button-up shirt and red tie to work in order to feel more important than he actually is. Today, he's overseeing a small staff of two teenagers: Sean, a glue-sniffer on loan from the massive juvenile detention center outside town; and Angela (her friends call her Angie), a sweet all-American girl of Hispanic descent.

"Got danggit, Sean!" Mr. Newton yells at the red-headed slacker with freckles and braces. "How much cheap cologne did you douse yourself with this morning? You're smelling up the whole place!"

"You don't like it, Mr. Newton?" Sean replies obliviously. "It's supposed to smell like CK1."

"Smells like an alley cat pissed in your eye!" Mr. Newton exclaims.

Angie snickers from behind the cappuccino machine, where she's pumping mud and milk foam.

"I'm afraid I have to side with the Boss Man this time," she teases her co-worker. "Maybe next time you don't use the whole bottle, huh?"

Sean and Angie are wearing matching uniforms: blue polo shirts and visors emblazoned with the company logo (a capital S and a capital J inside a bootlegged Superman shield). Brown aprons hang down below the knees of their khakis.

It's Friday, just after 10 am, meaning the morning rush is way over and three luckier employees have already gone home for the day. Just a few more hours standing in between most hard-working folks and a well-deserved weekend. Super Java's thinning out quickly. Only a mix of regulars and newcomers, all preparing to face whatever rewards or indignities lay ahead.

There's a married couple: Laurie and her husband Zack (better known as Sgt. Gallagher). It's a big day: Sgt. Gallagher's just returned home from a stint in the Middle East where he's been fighting for our freedom. Laurie brought him to Super Java because everyone in town knows they give a 50% discount to our heroes and first responders. The couple's playing with their two-and-a-half-year-old daughter, Abby. It's lovely!

Nearby, a good-looking bookworm named Venus is reading some kind of romance novel about handsome vampires. She's a regular at Super Java, stopping in daily between her college classes.

Angela's older brother Raul (nineteen--years-old) is also a regular. In fact, he used to work at Super Java with his sister and Mr. Newton. He left for greener pastures, now working as a valet at Che' LaBeef while attending the same college Venus goes to. The tips for parking luxury cars, trucks, and SUVs are way better than those from coffee patrons (and it's less of a drag than putting up with Mr. Newton). Raul comes in at least every Friday for Double Coco Bon-Bon Bombs.

When Angie gets off work in a couple more hours, the siblings plan on visiting their parents at the migrant detention center outside town.

"Do you promise they won't send Mom and Dad back to Mexico?" Angela asked her big brother earlier that morning for what must be the thousandth time.

"Don't worry, sis," Raul told her. "Hopefully, things will change when the new guy gets elected."

They're too young to be dealing with issues this serious on their own. But life's cruel, and very often to the innocent. And sometimes, it doesn't matter if you're a desperate dreamer or a privileged princess—sometimes, you're just in the wrong place at the wrong time (or even just the wrong color).

None of the other regulars or randoms adding to the coffeehouse's friendly din deserve much description or consideration, for reasons that will very soon become apparent. But there's someone who definitely stands out; a well-dressed loner with slicked-back hair. He's wearing an Armani suit and a gold Rolex on his wrist. Unlike Sean, he actually smells like he's wearing some decent cologne.

This suave stranger's feeling pretty good about himself (at least outwardly). Not only are his rich mom and dad recently deceased, he was able to cheat his brother and sisters out of their share of their inheritance. He got the land *and* the farm, flipping them for a fast buck from a shady ganja farmer at a fraction of their value.

The stranger looks down at his Rolex and, more importantly, his reflection in the glass. He smiles and winks at himself.

"No one can stop you now," he whispers, "you handsome dog!"

The second hand on the Rolex stalls, then clicks backward a few notches before resuming its normal course around the dial. The stranger doesn't care much about that. He knows the watch is fake (just like the Armani suit). And that's just fine.

The illusion of wealth will be good enough to dupe the rubes, is what this stranger's thinking. He's headed up to Atlantic City to make his millions. He'll be an actual high roller in no time. All he has to do is fake it 'til he makes it.

On his way east, he plans on stopping at every sleazy truck-stop saloon that doubles as a backdoor bordello. He wants to sample the elite amphetamines of each new town he drives through. He wants to go on a bender-adventure that'll leave every common conman and pimp from Stockton to Buffalo green with envy.

The stranger's nearing the bottom of his Extra-Large Brazilian Yerba Kombucha CBD Blast, almost ready to take a piss and hit the road. But as he's gulping his trendy brew, the paper cup and all of its contents explode into a fine mist with a powerful CRACK.

"What the fuck?" he hollers, ears ringing, face and clothes splattered with coffee.

He turns to behold an unholy spectacle.

Four masked madmen, armed to the gills.

* * *

"Here's the plan..." Papa Corn and his gang are huddled up in the back of the circus van. "Mister Blister, you're on crowd control."

Mister Blister exhales a cloud of cigarette smoke and nods once.

"Mister Jumbo, I want you to contain the staff."

Jumbo yips and salutes.

"Mister Noodledome, you wrangle the hostages into the back of the van—and help yourself to some tasty pastries."

Noodledome smiles big.

"Now then..." Papa Corn looks at his boys with pride. "It's showtime!"

Time seems to slow down when the sliding door on the side of the van opens. The clowns emerge, heavily armed in broad daylight, moving in unison like a pack of reservoir dogs. Scary as hell and cool as fuck.

Each clown pulls a hockey mask over his face. It's something special for the day's grand affair, certain to add an uncanny layer to the impending ultraviolence. Each mask is custom painted to match the unique face of the clown who wears it. They're clowns, wearing masks, painted like clowns. Papa loves irony.

A cowbell above the door of Super Java rings as the clowns file in. Before anyone has time to take notice, Mister Blister raises his .44 Magnum and blasts a cup of coffee out of some yuppy's hand. There's a lit cigarette sticking out of one of the mouth-holes in his mask.

"What the fuck?" the yuppy hollers, his greasy porno mustache dripping caffeinated foam.

Gasping! Screaming!

There's a hint of pandemonium before the masked Noodledome shoots his sawed-off shotgun at the ceiling, shocking everyone into silence. The customers cower up against walls and under tables.

A brave idiot makes a run for the side exit.

Mister Blister puts a bullet into the back of his head before he even touches the handle. His skull and brains drip down the glass door as his lifeless body hits the ground.

A quick-thinking uppity woman tries to dial 911, but Mister Blister blasts the cellphone out of her hand as she raises it to her ear. The shattered phone and several fingers hit the ground. Mister Blister would've left it at that, but the "Karen" screams, so he has to finish her off.

"Crowd control," Mister Blister mutters, exhaling a cloud of cigarette smoke through the holes in his hockey mask.

Sgt. Gallagher stands up in between the clowns and his family.

Papa Corn steps forward, confronting the soldier while lifting his mask up.

"Hello fine sir... My name is Papa Corn, but my friends call me... Papa Corn! And who do I have the pleasure of meeting?"

"I am Sgt. Zack Gallagher of the United States Army." He holds his hands up so Papa can see he's unarmed.

"Well, Mister Sgt. Zack Gallagher of the United States Army, it is an honor and a pleasure to meet you. On behalf of my esteemed associates and myself, I would like to thank you from the bottom of my heart for your service and contribution to our great country." Papa extends his gloved hand for a shake.

"Let's just leave this like it is," Sgt. Gallagher pleads. "You and your friends can leave here without anyone else getting hurt."

Papa corn contemplates.

"You're right. He's right, you know?" Papa tells his crew.

"There's just too much violence in the world today. And

trust me when I say I've seen my share over there." Sgt. Gallagher speaks with genuine emotion and empathy.

Papa Corn looks dejected.

"I'm truly sorry. And you know, you're 100% right. If we can't love better than a third world country, then we really aren't any better than they are." Papa's sounding downright somber. He's still extending his right hand towards the Sgt. for a shake.

This time Sgt. Gallagher reluctantly complies and begins to shake Papa's gloved hand.

Papa smiles, beaming with big puppy dog eyes. Then, using his left hand, he procures his .45 and presses it against the Sgt.'s forehead.

"Happy trails."

He pulls the trigger and splits Sgt. Gallagher's head in half. Blood and brain-matter combine into a confetti-mist of reds and grays.

Laurie screams in unfathomable terror and holds Abby tight to her bosom. The other patrons and employees are terrified by this senseless act of violence.

Noodledome (eating a sprinkle-covered doughnut) laughs loud and uncontrollably.

"I'm proud to be an American, for at least I know I'm free..." Papa sings. "Well G.I. Joe, you are definitely free now. Tell St. Peter I'm bringing bolt cutters to the gate with me!"

"You monster! Why would you do that?" grief-stricken Laurie screams at Papa.

"I know, you're right..." Papa replies. "Like I'm going to Heaven anyways... My ass will be burning in Hell with Mister Blister."

Mister Blister shrugs his shoulders in response.

"Friends, Romans, countrymen, lend me your *rears*..." Papa commands. "I require your complete attention!"

Mr. Newton and Sean consider sneaking out the back (fuck the customers), but masked Jumbo hops up on the counter, a heavy chrome six-shooter in each tiny hand. They freeze (along with Angela, who's also been watching the insanity from behind the counter).

"¡No, no, no... Papá está hablando pendejos!" the mini-masked clown scolds the employees.

"All eyes on me," Papa Corn continues as Mister Blister and Noodledome continue to stalk the coffeehouse: "Please forgive our sudden intrusion into your mundane lives. I assure you, it's nothing personal."

Whimpering, Venus draws Papa Corn's attention, sending his saliva glands into overdrive.

"My, my, my..." Papa Corn lifts his mask and smiles at the young woman, picking up her book. "I've read this one... It's definitely not as good as the first one. Bella and Edward break up."

Venus shivers.

Papa puts his mask back down and addresses his captive audience at large again,

"If everyone does exactly as I say, when I say, I promise everything will be A-okay!"

"Just take the money in the register!" Mr. Newton yells. "And in the safe. I'll give you the combination. No one else needs to get hurt!"

Papa Corn zeroes in on the manager.

"We don't want your money, silly man... Besides, don't you know that money's the root of all evil? And do we look evil to you?" Papa teases him. "Mister Noodledome, if you'd be so generous..."

To illustrate the point, Noodledome turns to the cash register and shoots the shit out of it with both barrels of his sawed-off shotgun. "KABOOM!" Jumbo quickly ducks and takes cover as machinery, coins, and shredded bills fly.

Mr. Newton holds firm, but Sean and Angie tremble behind his back.

"I said I don't want any trouble... no one else needs to get hurt!" Mr. Newton struggles to speak.

Noodledome hoots hysterically.

"You don't say, do you?" Papa grins. "Well... you're in luck. We're not 'trouble' at all. We're the opposite... Consider us liberation and freedom from your pathetic existence."

Mr. Newton looks dumbfounded.

Papa grabs him by his collar.

"You can think of me like Saint Michael the Archangel... and I'm the leader of the Army of God, the leader of Heaven's forces in their triumph over the powers of Hell..." Papa stares deep into his eyes. "And as for no one needing to get hurt," Papa reads the manager's name tag, "Teddy... I'm afraid that simply isn't true."

"What do you want, then?" Mr. Newton asks.

"What we want," Papa Corn addresses the crowd at large again, "is quite simple, actually. We want some of you to come with us." If they could see beneath his mask, they'd see he's smiling. His voice, even muffled, is almost soothing, making his next sentence all the more chilling. "The rest of you, I'm afraid—will have to die."

Raul closes his eyes and prays quietly.

"Bullshit!" the cocky, ballsy, over-caffeinated stranger suddenly declares, standing up at his table.

"Sit down, asshole!" Mister Blister barks, blowing smoke and cocking his pistol. He wants to kill this fucking yuppy real bad.

The goliath Noodledome grabs the stranger by the back of his shirt and slams him back into his seat.

"Now," Papa says, "let's make this snappy!"

* * *

After assassinating every last unlucky motherfucking customer at Super Java, Papa Corn, Mister Blister, and Jumbo, fall upon the staff. (Noodledome's busy carrying the "lucky" hostages to the van). The clowns aim their guns at the Super Java crew, sending Mr. Newton into an impassioned Hail Mary.

"Please!" he says with open arms, his employees hiding behind his back. "You don't have to do this. You can let us live!"

Behind his mask, Jumbo's panting like a thirsty dog, raring to bust some caps.

"Tell me, Teddy," Papa Corn replies. "Why do you three deserve to live when everyone else has just been ruthlessly mowed down? Are you somehow... special?"

Sean whimpers.

"Hey man! I'm not like those hipster losers out there, man," he explains. "I just work here! I like clowns, dude!"

Papa Corn and Mister Blister exchange sideways glances and a silent chuckle. The employee's willingness to bite the hands that feed him is commendable.

"Shut up, Sean!" Mr. Newton snaps. "We're apparently dealing with psychopaths without remorse!"

"Assuming I accept your argument, Teddy," Papa says, "and we do decide to take you with us what makes you so certain that what awaits you won't be worse?"

"Worse than being gunned down in cold blood?" Mr. Newton replies. "I'll take that chance!"

Papa Corn smiles.

"Mister Blister, Jumbo, please take these three to the van."

His henchmen comply, pushing the trio towards the front door.

"The Babysitter will be busy tonight..." Papa whispers.

* * *

The clowns remove their blood-splattered hockey masks.

Noodledome's behind the wheel of the van, racing out of town, headed towards the Chihuahuan Desert. He's chomping on a Moon-Pie, feeling delightful. The day's off to a splendid start.

Several police cars, lights flashing, sirens screaming, speed past the circus van going the opposite direction.

Noodledome laughs.

Papa Corn's sitting shotgun, scanning the AM radio for a local news station. He stops when a voice emerges from the static.

"...This is Coyote Jack reporting for AM 1566 and we're getting breaking news out of Brownsville...."

Papa Corn sits back as the report continues.

"Police are responding to reports of a massacre at the local Super Java. Eyewitnesses to the aftermath say at least ten people are dead, with no apparent survivors..."

Papa Corn and Noodledome smile proudly at one another.

The radio continues,

"...Four suspects, described as members of a disco band wearing matching Leatherface masks, were seen fleeing the scene with several hostages. Authorities are on the lookout for a yellow van..."

Mister Blister and Jumbo are wrestling with the hostages in the back of the van. Blister binds their wrists and ankles with zip-ties while Jumbo fits everyone with a fresh duct-tape muzzle. They've done this shit a thousand times.

"Easy there, buster!" the stranger complains as the smoking clown roughs him up.

"It's Blister!" Mister Blister replies harshly, blowing smoke in the yuppy's face. "If it was up to me, I'd make an ashtray outta your esophagus."

Gagged and bound, Raul and Angie regard each other apprehensively. The clowns don't know that the two of them are related; the fact that they were both selected for kidnapping was a complete coincidence. And while each is relieved that the other survived the massacre, there is no relief.

An ominous fate awaits them all.

CHAPTER 3

LA NIÑERO (THE BABYSITTER)

It's been a month since Papa Corn and company conscripted Hugo. As expected, he's excelled throughout every aspect of Papa's program. In fact, he's on track to become The Valedictorian of "Getting Shit Handled".

Outwardly, there's nary a trace of the ice-cream man who was. Hugo's become something else: The Babysitter. And, if he passes his final test, proves himself worthy of transcendence, he'll metamorphosize once again—into something new!

The Babysitter lost his mind when he lost his balls. The shock and pain (while in the throes of psychedelic delirium) were more than his brain could recover from. As such, he was like fresh putty in Papa Corn's hands.

He doesn't even talk anymore.

The Babysitter's body's different now too, also due to his agonizing de-masculation. Without testosterone, his estrogen levels surged, resulting in a set of pendulous man-tits. He was always rotund; now, he's absolutely "prison swollen" and strong as fuck.

Papa Corn and Noodledome collaborated on perfecting The Babysitter's new look and persona. Since he's clearly anything but, they thought dressing him up as a schoolboy was hilarious. Also ironic, considering Schoolboy used to be one of the ice-cream man's favorite Super-Secret-Special Flavors.

The Babysitter's huge, but everything he wears is short: short-sleeved button-up shirt, short black tie, and short black shorts that end mid-thigh. Black suspenders keep his shorts hiked up over his bellybutton. Short black socks and black dress-shoes complete the look.

The juxtaposition between the man and the outfit's amusing, but The Babysitter's mask turns everything on its head: blank, round, and yellowed by time; cheeks are bloated like a baby, mouth and eyes are tight and pensive. He's an abomination with a cracked porcelain face. Humorless, merciless, and ineffable.

When it was time for The Babysitter to choose a signature weapon, the machete seemed an obvious and fitting choice.

But Papa Corn disagreed.

"There are already too many slashers," he complained. "Besides, he's a bruiser. He's a smasher!"

Papa concluded that The Babysitter should wield the very same sledgehammer that scrambled his huevos. Papa loves irony.

The Babysitter's in his room right now. It's a box. Actually, it's a hollowed-out industrial refrigeration unit. It's where he rests, surrounded by absolute darkness, in between his lessons. The box is wrapped in chains, for everyone else's safety *and* his own.

Yet he stirs, restless; his excitement and psychosis rising. Tonight's the big hunt. It's almost time!

* * *

The chloroform's starting to wear off and the hostages are stirring.

The "dapper" stranger's the first one to fully regain consciousness.

"Ah... fuck..." he groans, holding his head in his hands and wobbling onto his feet. His eyes need time to adjust to the dark. "Where the fuck am I?" he mutters.

A scream pierces the swirling haze.

"Abby!" Laurie screams. "Abby! Where's my baby? Where's my baby?""

Her cries bring everyone else back from unconsciousness; they struggle to shake off heavy waves of grogginess.

"Where's my baby!"

Venus knows Laurie casually from the coffeehouse; she moves in to console the distraught mother.

"Angie!" Raul finds his sister and hugs her close.

"Where are we, Raul?" she asks.

Raul looks around and cranes his neck.

"I don't know, sis... something about this place feels familiar."

"Shit, kid," the stranger interjects. "If you've been here before, I feel sorry for you."

They're in a large, dilapidated grocery store that doubled as a Tex/Mex Flea Market. For you history buffs, it was once called "La Guadalupana". The structure's size and the hostages' position in relation to any exit, is unknown. This place may have once been functional, beautiful even. But now, it's something straight out of a horror movie.

Mr. Newton reconnects with his employees to assess their predicament.

"Sean, Angie... are you kid alright?"

"I want to go back to juvie," Sean replies. "Fuck being sober."

"I'm scared, Mr. Newton," Angie says, still holding onto her brother

"Hey! Check it out..." Raul says excitedly. "There's a box of flashlights here."

"Out of my way there, amigo," the stranger demands. "Give me one of those!"

In addition to flashlights, the box contains canned foods, cereal, baby formula, diapers, old toys, and a black ventriloquist puppet holding a cardboard sign that says, "*My name is ~~Kunta~~ Toby*".

The crappy vintage flashlights are distributed. The stranger hits his flashlight a few times, hoping it'll shine brighter.

"Work you piece of shit!"

"¡Es muy pendejo!" says Raul.

"Abby!" Laurie's frantic. "Where are you, baby? Abby! Abby!"

The cold sound of metal chains hitting the concrete floor emanates from within, echoing throughout the warehouse.

"Wait a fucking minute... Son of a bitch!" the stranger suddenly yells. "Which one of you assholes took my watch?"

Who the hell is this guy? Mr. Newton wonders.

"Let me get this straight," he replies. "We've all just been kidnapped by a pack of murderous deviant clowns—and you think one of *us* took your goddamn watch?"

"It's not just a goddamn watch!" the stranger retorts. "It was a fucking Rolex!" He straightens his sport coat as if to illustrate his innate superiority to the rest of them.

"Hey man," Raul says, "don't you think you have more important things to worry about right now?"

Angie's holding her brother's hand and standing close.

"Yeah, don't be an elitest dickhead." She chides.

The stranger huffs.

"Look *Chica*..." he gets up on his high horse, "I don't know what kind of cartel bullshit you spicks have gotten yourselves into and, frankly, I don't give two fucks about any of y'all! All I know is it's got nothing to do with me." He looks around the room. "The only thing I care about is M and E. Me and My Existence. I'm Audi Five Thousand. See ya, don't wanna be ya!"

He's about to plumb the surrounding darkness when a crackling ragtime tune starts playing over the indoor PA system—at maximum volume. The system begins feeding back on itself. Everyone's holding their hands over their ears and cringing. Thankfully, the sonic assault lets up.

"Ladies and gentlemen..." Papa Corn's voice comes over the speakers, sounding canned and compressed, like an old radio. "Welcome—to the Greatest Show on Earth!"

Galla music blasts throughout the warehouse.

"Where the fuck is my baby?" Laurie shrieks at the disembodies voice (which, of course, ignores her).

"The name of the game is... Survive the Night!"

Noodledome can be heard laughing maniacally in the background.

"It's pretty straightforward," Papa continues. "You have until daylight to escape from this place. Of course, you'll all be chaperoned by... The Babysitter!"

Venus, who's been struggling to wrap her mind around this entire situation, begins to whimper.

Angie holds her brother tight.

Sean pees his pants, but just a little bit.

"I probably shouldn't be saying this..." Papa's voice has them all frozen, "and I only do so in the hopes of motivating you to reach your full potentials. But, frankly..." he chuckles, "if everything goes as we suspect, all of you will be dead by dawn."

Noodledome's insane laugh hits a higher octave.

The hostages are shaken.

"There are no rules beyond surviving... doing whatever it takes to see another day. Creativity and ingenuity are encouraged, so by all means, give it your best shot. Feel free to think outside the box! And before you fret, don't you ever forget—that Papa loves you... Papa will always love you..."

Jumbo can be heard yipping and yapping as Papa Corn ends his transmission.

Mariachi music begins to play, and will continue to do so, on loop, for the rest of the night.

The stranger's the first to speak.

"Welp, that cinches it. I'm getting' the fuck outta here!"

"Wait a minute now," Mr. Newton steps up. "Don't you think it's best if we stick together? Strength in numbers? Who knows what's waiting for us inside there?"

"I don't know, and I don't care!" the stranger huffs. "I'm not afraid of clowns... or this babysitter—whoever *she* is. Besides, you all'd probably slow me down." He shines his flashlight forward and starts off into the unknown.

"Wait!" Venus shouts after him.

"Don't leave us, dude!" Sean pleads.

"Sorry ladies," he replies callously. "I'm a lone wolf." He takes a breath, throws his head back, and howls while walking away. He's gone.

"Screw that guy," Raul says. "We don't need him."

"What should we do?" Angie asks. "Mr. Newton—do you have a plan?"

"Well," Mr. Newton puts his hands on his hips. "Number one, we have *got* to stay together. Number two, everyone *needs* to remain calm. Number three..."

Venus screams and points into the nebulous darkness.

Everyone struggles to peer into the valley of shadows. The hostages are aghast to see a vast blob bumbling towards them. Its features become more apparent the closer it gets.

"Hello?" Mr. Newton calls out nervously. "Are you one of them?"

Raul looks at Mr. Newton.

"Let's not chance it! Let's just get out of here," he whispers.

"Well, wait a second," Mr. Newton replies. "It's not a clown. Just a big... fat... man?"

Reeling with confusion, no one moves as The Babysitter continues towards them. His size is intimidating, but there's something disarming about his slow, deliberate movements.

"What's he holding, Mr. Newton?" Sean asks.

"Oh my God," Mr. Newton replies, shocked.

"Abby!" Laurie yells.

The Babysitter removes his hand from little Abby's mouth; the toddler screams and begins to struggle.

Laurie explodes with emotion and leaps into action like a mama grizzly bear.

"Are you crazy?" Mr. Newton hisses. "Get back here!"

"Laurie, no!" Venus shouts.

Time seems to slow down.

The Babysitter sits the child down on the dirty concrete floor. Then he reaches over his shoulder, retrieving his sledge-hammer from its back sheath.

Like a fastball from a Major League Baseball player, Laurie comes barreling in to save her daughter.

The Babysitter cocks back his hammer.

The other hostages tremble, holding their collective breath.

Here batta, batta...

The Babysitter swings his hammer down, obliterating Laurie's cranium. The force causes her to bite off her tongue; her eyes pop out of her head. The vertebrae in her neck compress and shatter. A clump of her skull, skin, and hair remains stuck to the hammer when The Babysitter puts it back over his shoulder.

Broken Laurie crumples to the ground—fodder for Noodledome's next work of art.

Bedlam!

So much for staying together. So much for staying calm.

Venus runs off alone, screaming and gagging. Raul pulls his sobbing sister down another corridor by her arm. Sean's definitely peeing his pants as he and Mr. Newton hightail it down another hallway all together.

The game's afoot.

* * *

The Babysitter's just about as cruel and powerful as anyone you'll never want to come across. But he's not fast. He'd be an ineffectual hunter in the out-of-doors (or, at the very least, he'd have a shamefully low kill-count). He's got no hustle.

He was lucky to have knocked off the first player so easily; lucky he had the right bait to catch a mama bear. But he'll never get that lucky again—not tonight, at least.

The setting, this dreary indoor expanse, is key to The Babysitter's advantage. His prey can only run so far before, inevitably, becoming cornered. But darkness, stealth, and a sledgehammer aren't the only tools in The Babysitter's arsenal. The warehouse teems with tricks and traps.

The Babysitter isn't the only monster prowling in the gloom. There are... others.

The survivors of the ice-cream man's last hurrah now call this dungeon their home. Since their "rescue" from the back of the truck, these children have been locked inside the labyrinth, left to their own devices.

Their minds have been warped by Papa's program. 1970s-era pornos are projected on the walls and ceilings. Scenes of hairy men and women, sideways dicks and floppy tits, butts and gushers play continuously, incessantly.

They've survived by eating the bodies of the kids who died in the back of the ice-cream truck, but all that's left is a pile of bones and gristle. The children have developed a taste for human flesh—and they're ravenous!

They're no longer human. They have no memories of their lives before the dungeon. They're feral.

The Babysitter doesn't diddle anymore, but he still wants to murder these lost girls and boys; he still delights in their screams and suffering. Recent days and nights have been spent engaging in festive bouts of cat and mice. But tonight, The Babysitter's got bigger fish to fry.

The stranger's been strutting around the maddening maze for hours, dodging bear-traps, pendulums, and tripwires by the seat of his pants. It's a combination of situational awareness and dumb luck. But he's no closer to locating egress, and he's starting to get frustrated.

He hears someone crying in the darkness and goes to investigate. He finds Venus cowering in a corner, attempting to hide behind a pile of wooden crates and cardboard boxes. She screams when the stranger approaches.

"Keep it down, ya banshee!" he scolds. "It's me!"

"Have you found a way out?" Venus asks, snot dripping down her nose.

"Does it look like I found a way out?" the stranger snaps. "I'm still here, aren't I?"

"Come hide with me!" she begs.

"Hell no!" the stranger replies. "There's gotta be a way out somewhere."

"Take me with you, please!"

The stranger's about to tell this sorority sister where to stick it, when it occurs to him; she might be useful.

"Sure," he says with a half-smile. "As long as you do what I say, you can come with me."

"Okay," Venus whimpers.

"Good. Now let's go. You first."

Well, it isn't long before the stranger begins to think Venus is more trouble than she's worth. Sure, she can help clear the way for him; she turns corners first, ensuring the coast is clear. She'll be the first to meet the business-end of a sledgehammer.

But God damn, is she annoying! Stifling screams, shivering like a scared dog, complaining every step of the damn way. He's considering ditching her again when they come across a wall with a hole in it, just about big enough to squeeze through.

"Stick your head in there and tell me what you see," the stranger commands.

Venus grudgingly agrees, leaning in and looking into the gray haze on the other side.

"I-I don't see anything," she reports.

"Can you squeeze through?"

"Let me try..."

As Venus struggles, the stranger attempts to push her through.

"Stop!" she yells when her hips get wedged. "I'm stuck!" Her legs are kicking in the air; her top half struggles on the other side of the wall. "Pull me out!"

The stranger tries to yank Venus back, but she's lodged good.

Venus screams.

Suddenly, something rips her out of the stranger's hands and pulls her through the wall. He listens in horror to the sounds of a violent struggle. There's a sickening crunch before everything behind the wall goes quiet.

The stranger stands frozen, momentarily uncertain what to do next.

Without warning, The Babysitter smashes through the wall like The Kool-Aid Man, like The Incredible Hulk. His hammer's dripping with Venus's fresh blood.

"Holy shit!" the stranger hollers before dashing away down another dark corridor.

Is he sad about what happened to poor Venus? Not one bit.

Better her than me! The stranger thinks as he bolts off into the darkness.

* * *

After hours of wandering the corridors, surviving by the skin of their teeth, Mr. Newton and Sean run into the stranger in what might have been a locker room.

"Well, well," Mr. Newton says. "If it isn't Daddy Warbucks."

The stranger sneers, but secretly likes the comparison.

"Not so easy finding a way out on your own, it seems."

"Like you Bozos are doing any better," the stranger retorts.

"Have you seen anyone else?" Sean asks.

"I ran into that Barbie. Things didn't work out too well for her, I'm afraid."

"She's dead?" Mr. Newton gasps. "What happened?"

"Never mind the details," the stranger replies. "You shitheads can tag along with me if you like. Just don't get in my way." He sniffs the air and looks at Sean. "By the way, kid. You fucking stink!"

After a minor setback involving a nail piercing the bottom of Sean's shoe and foot, the three are once again pushing forward.

"God damn!" the stranger complains. "If that maniac couldn't already smell you, he definitely *heard* you screaming like a puss back there."

"It fucking hurt!" Sean replies, moping and limping. "I'm gonna have to get a tetanus shot."

A few minutes later, the trio come across an exit sign. Not an actual EXIT sign, just the word *"EXIT"* spray-painted on a wall at the end of a corridor (with a crooked arrow pointing left into liminal space).

"Let's go!" Sean says with excitement.

"Not so fast," Mr. Newton cautions. "It might be a trap."

Suddenly, it doesn't matter.

They hear heavy footsteps coming up behind them. They turn. It's The Babysitter!

"Run!" Mr. Newton yells, hustling down the corridor towards the *"EXIT"* followed by Sean and the stranger.

The Babysitter doesn't chase them. Instead, he pulls an automatic garage door opener out of his pocket. With the push of a button, a volley of mounted stun-guns eject upon the players as they run.

By sheer luck, the fishhooks on wires miss Sean and the stranger.

Mr. Newton isn't so lucky. He's got prods in his face, on his neck, and on his ass. Thousands of incapacitating volts pump through the crimped wires into the man's body.

He seizes, crackles, and twitches before falling limp, life dripping out of him, smoke wafting from his open mouth.

Just as suddenly as the stun-guns deployed, a pack of filthy, rabid children flood the corridor, swarming Mr. Newton's body. They gnash their teeth and claw their finger-nails into the man's guts and eye-sockets. They glut them-selves on chunks of meat and organs, drenching their hands and faces.

In his last moments, Mr. Newton wishes he'd opted for a quick death back at Super Java.

Sean's stupefied with fear.

"Snap out of it, dipshit!" the stranger yells, yanking Sean along by his scruff.

The duo turns the corner. There's another *"EXIT"* sign above what appears to be a door. But it's not a door.

"Come on!" Sean screams, suddenly on overdrive, running at full speed. As he gets closer, he realizes with dread that what he thought was a door is actually just a painted yellow rectangle. But painted with what?

Sean's running too fast to slow down. He slams into the decoy door with a thud, making hard contact with the side of his head, his chest, crotch, and legs. The shock causes his body to wilt—but he doesn't fall. He's stuck!

"What the fuck?" the young man whines. He tries to extract himself, but it's no use. He isn't held in place by any household glue or epoxy. Whatever coats the wall is thick, industrial—and it burns. Sean's stuck like a bug on human flypaper.

"Help me!" he screams, thrashing desperately, causing his cheek to stretch unnaturally. "Help me! It hurts!"

The stranger grabs Sean by the back of his shirt and gives him a few good tugs. Nope. He isn't going anywhere.

"Help me!"

"I'm trying," the stranger replies half-heartedly.

But now, it's too late.

Calm and ominous, The Babysitter's bearing down on them, one chunky step at a time.

The stranger pulls his trademark maneuver and bails.

"Sorry, kid," he says, feeling anything but sorry. "He's all yours!" he yells towards The Babysitter before scampering away deeper into the dungeon.

As he moves away, he can hear the sounds of The Babysitter... swinging his hammer down on Sean's body. God only knows what remains of him.

"Better you than me," the stranger mutters.

* * *

"Now I remember where we are!"

Raul and Angie find themselves in an indoor marketplace lined with barren booths. It's empty now, beyond disrepair. But it was once a lively hub for arts, crafts, food, and a million other things you never knew you needed.

"This is the flea market at La Guadalupana," Raul says. "Or at least it was. Mom used to take us here when we were kids. Remember?"

"No," Angie admits. "I must have been too young."

"Yeah, you were a baby." Raul allows himself a moment of nostalgia amid the horror. "That's where they had puppet shows, and that's where they had Virgin Mary statues; and the best Elote ever from a guy with a food-cart over there..."

Raul and Angie are startled by a voice coming up behind them.

"Great!" It's the stranger. "Point me in the direction of a velvet Jesus painting," he scoffs condescendingly.

"Where did you come from?" Raul asks suspiciously.

"Same as you," the stranger replies, "Just wandering around this Indiana Jones ride, trying to find a way out."

"Have you seen anyone else?" Angie asks hopefully.

"No... can't say that I have," he replies.

"What about the monster man?" she inquires.

"That fat tub who moves like a glacier?" The stranger chuckles. "I'm not afraid of that guy."

Raul and Angie roll their eyes.

"Nonetheless," the stranger continues. "I think I've had my fill of this... experience. You said you been here before, right, kid?"

"Yeah, that's right," Raul replies.

"So... how do we get out of here?"

Raul thinks for a minute.

"If this is the main marketplace, then the loading docks should be over there," he points into the darkness.

The Mariachi music cuts out.

"And then there were three..." It's Papa Corn's canned voice coming over the intercom. "It's almost dawn and, by fate or good fortune, you're all still alive."

"Fuck you, Ronald McDonald!" the stranger screams at the ceiling.

"Of course, you only get to live if you make it all the way outside. You might be getting close," they can hear Noodle-dome's grating laughter in the background, "but so is The Babysitter. And I'm afraid you three have made him very... angry!"

"Come on!" Raul says, "Let's get going."

"This is Papa Corn, signing off. Happy trails... Until we meet again..."

The music returns, but instead of Mariachi, it's hectic techno playing at an uncomfortable volume.

"Look!" Angie screams, pointing into the darkness behind them.

It's The Babysitter, fuming, focused, ready to complete his mission. Like a hippopotamus on dry land, he charges... slowly.

Raul grabs his little sister by her shoulders.

"Listen to me!" He's dead serious. "I want you to run! Go with that tech-bro and get out of here!"

"What are you talking about?" Angie replies, tearing up.

"I love you, Angie. Tell mom and dad I love them too."

Emotional orchestral chords seem to swell around them, elevating them beyond their gruesome circumstances. Time seems to slow down.

Raul turns to face The Babysitter. He grabs a loose two-by-four from the ground and holds it like a baseball bat.

"Come and get me fuckface!" Raul releases a war cry before charging the abominable monolith.

"No!" Angie screams as the stranger pulls her away from the immediate danger.

Raul and The Babysitter collide with an impressive amount of kinetic fury. Still, the teenager's no match for the madman, like a bug going up against the windshield of a speeding Camero. At least Raul's death is an honorable one; quick and relatively painless.

Angie's hysterical as the stranger drags her towards the loading docks.

"Let me go!" she cries.

"Not a chance!" the stranger replies angrily.

As they tear through the booths and barricades, they come across the mummified body of a dead Boy Scout. It's the kind of sight that could take a person's breath away, cripple them emotionally. But Angie and the stranger have seen so much horror over the past twenty hours, it barely even registers.

The stranger and Angie finally arrive at the loading dock. There are six bays for trucks and semis, but they're all closed; rolling metal doors are secured with massive padlocks.

"God damn!" The stranger sizes up the situation, evaluating his options. He sees fire-escape doors, but the handles are locked with a coil of rusty chains. There's an open air duct, but that leads back into The Babysitter's insane dominion. There's an industrial-sized incinerator filled with decades of melted plastic and ash up against a wall.

"What are we gonna do?" Angie cries, distraught.

The stranger has an idea.

"I don't know what *you're* gonna do, kid. But I know exactly what *I'm* gonna do!" He holds Angie's arms behind her back.

"What are you doing?" she yells. "That hurts! Let me go!"

"Hey, Lard-Ass!" the stranger calls into the darkness. "I've got a surprise for you!"

Angie's confused and terrified.

"What are you doing!" she screeches. "He'll find us!"

"That's what I'm hoping for!" The stranger's using her as bait. "Hey! Moby Dick! Where are you hiding?"

Speak of the Devil and he might just appear.

The Babysitter emerges from the darkness.

The stranger puts a hand over Angie's mouth to keep her from screaming.

"Hey big guy!" The stranger smiles. "Let's say you and me make a deal?"

The Babysitter stops.

"You can have her!" the stranger tells the beast. "Shit, if she's not enough, I've got a Rolex. You can have that, too!"

The Babysitter moves in. Killing just one of them, at this point, would be nothing short of anti-climactic.

But the stranger wasn't really using Angie as a bargaining chip—just an object, a tool, something to give him a bit of extra time.

"Come and get her, Grimace!" He tosses screaming, frantic Angie directly into The Babysitter's clutches. He doesn't wait to watch the bloodbath unfold—the sound of it's bad enough. With The Babysitter momentarily occupied, the stranger dives into the giant incinerator. From inside, he closes the heavy metal door. He's instantly coated in soot and black mold.

"Incinerators have chimneys," he mutters to himself, crawling about through the debris, looking upward. "Incinerators have chimneys..."

Angie screams no more, but the usually silent ogre's fussing, grunting, and growling.

Having demolished the girl, The Babysitter's confused and enraged at not being able to find his final victim. He looks around frantically, desperately, finally noticing the massive machine in the corner.

He stumbles forward, drops his sledgehammer, and pulls the heavy metal door of the incinerator open. But whereas the stranger was able to wriggle inside with ease, it would be easier for an elephant to fuck a pig than for The Babysitter to follow.

The monster-man thrusts his powerful arm inside the incinerator.

The stranger hollers when The Babysitter grabs his ankle. "Let go of me, Shrek!" With a swift kick, he's able to escape the grasp of The Babysitter. "Fuck you, Tweedle Dumb-Dumb!"

The Babysitter reels. He's beside himself, panicking, running in circles. He's almost out of time!

He notices the control panel on the wall beside the incinerator. That's it! If he can't crush the last player with his sledgehammer, he'll burn him alive!

His fat, sweaty fingers tremble as he turns on the gas and presses down hard on the ignitor. Nothing. Just a loud CLICK. He pushes it again. Another CLICK and nothing else.

The Babysitter pauses, takes a deep breath, and says a silent prayer to Papa.

CLICK, and this time, a mighty WHOOSH follows as the gas inside the incinerator ignites.

Over the roar of the flames and the hissing of gas, The Babysitter can hear the stranger—screaming!

CHAPTER 4

EL MUNECO (DOLL BOY)

The sun's coming up in the East over the Gulf of Mexico. Birds are singing. Cold-blooded lizards are stirring.

A heavy metal door opens at the base of a towering smokestack. .

With a moderate amount of effort, the stranger stirs from within, emerging like a sweaty black sea lion. He coughs uncontrollably on his hands and knees, working hot ash and debris out of his lungs and windpipe. He spits. Then he hears the applause.

Not a lot of applause.

The stranger looks up to see Papa Corn, Mister Blister, Noodledome, and Jumbo sitting in a semicircle around the smoldering remains of a campfire. Empty bottles of whisky, bongs, crack pipes, and a couple of dead prostitutes attest to the fact that they've been there all night.

Little Abby sits close by. Calmed by trauma, she casually

toys with sticks and empty beer cans. With black and white greasepaint smeared across her face, she looks like the world's littlest Juggalo.

"Congratulations!" Papa Corn beams up at the stranger.

The applause ends.

The stranger stands up and regards the scene, simultaneously making a feeble effort to dust himself off.

"I must say," Papa continues, "this is a surprising turn of events. Mister Blister bet me a pack of cigarettes that you'd be the first to go. Consider me... impressed!"

Mister Blister nods, tossing Papa a half-empty box of Perro Azul Cigarrillos.

The clowns remain seated, regarding the stranger kindly.

Since he doesn't seem to be in any imminent peril, the stranger doesn't run. In fact, he feels downright emboldened.

"Well, that's what you get for underestimating me!" he replies.

The clowns keep looking at him, smiling.

"So, I guess I'm the winner then, right?" the stranger says. "I mean, isn't that how this sort of thing goes? I'm the last one to survive the night without getting killed or possessed by a ghost, or whatever, so I get the prize, right?"

Papa Corn smiles, amused.

"I suppose you're right—uh..." he pauses. "This is embarrassing, but it's only now occurring to me that we've never been formally introduced."

"I'm Brandon," the stranger says.

"Pleasure to meet you, Mister Brandon. My name is Papa Corn, but my friends call me... Papa Corn!"

The clowns all chuckle.

"So, tell me, Brandon," Papa says, "what kind of prize do you desire?"

"How about a thousand bucks?" Brandon replies. "At least enough to keep my dick wet from here to Alabama."

"How about something even better than money?" Papa counters. "How about a chance to learn what kind of man you *really* are? I must say, I found the depths you sank in the name of self-preservation to be quite impressive. What you did to that Hispanic girl..." Papa Corn gives a chef's kiss. "Bellissimo."

"No thanks. I'll take the thousand bucks."

"I'm sorry, Brandon," Papa says. "But look on the bright side." He stands up. "You won't need money where you're going."

The other clowns stand up. They slowly begin closing in on Brandon.

Brandon's getting nervous.

"What's going on here, guys?"

"I do have something for you, though." Papa Corn reaches into his coat pocket. "Consider it a consolation prize." He hands Brandon a gold object.

"Fuckin' a!" Brandon exclaims. "It's my fucking watch! Well, I guess it's better than a stick in the eye!" He nods his head. "Welp, see ya, wouldn't wanna—"

Mister Blister and Noodledome each stick an electric cattle-prod under one of Brandon's armpits. The lone survivor seizes and shudders before falling to the ground, completely unconscious.

"Jumbo, Noodledome. Please take Mister Brandon to the van."

The biggest clown and the smallest clown do as they're told. Little Abby toddles along after them.

"If he can survive a night with The Babysitter," Papa opines, "he might come in handy down the line..."

"What about The Babysitter?" Mister Blister asks while puffing on a cigarette. "We gonna cut him loose?"

Papa Corn sighs.

"It's true," Papa tells Blister, "He failed to complete the task *exactly* as commanded. He allowed someone to get away. Obviously, he isn't ready." Papa shakes his head and puts his hands on his hips. "I promised that poor boy that, after tonight, we'd never put him back in that box again. He won't be happy."

"Want me to take care of it, Boss?" Mister Blister offers. "Let the chips fall where they may?"

"No," Papa replies, more than slightly forlorn. "He's my special project. It should be me who does it."

"Suit yourself," Mister Blister replies. "See you back at the van."

* * *

Papa Corn finds his protégé sitting quietly on the loading dock floor.

The Babysitter's had quite a night. His arms are scratched and bitten, his clothes are torn and dirty, and his clay mask is cracked and stained with the blood of his victims. He hops to his feet when he sees Papa Corn, desperate for his master's approval.

Papa approaches slowly, his hands behind his back.

"I'm so proud of you," he beams at The Babysitter. "You really rose to the challenge. You proved that you can improvise. I'm so impressed with how far you've come!"

The Babysitter's elated, hooting like an orangutan. Beneath his mask, he's grinning like a child.

"Unfortunately..."

The Babysitter's heart drops.

"Unfortunately... you allowed one of them to get away. You know what that means..."

The Babysitter's devastated. He hates that he let Papa Corn down. He deserves to be punished! He falls to his knees, pantomiming his desire to have Papa beat him and kick him. He picks his bloody sledgehammer off the floor, offering it to Papa so he can break his bones.

Papa sighs.

"No, no. None of that will be necessary."

The Babysitter continues his displays of disappointment, banging his fists against his bald head and the concrete floor.

"Shh..." Papa soothes. "It's not as bad as all that. You've earned something, at least: a choice."

Papa Corn pulls his arms out from behind his back. In one hand, his favorite gun; in the other hand, The Babysitter's shackles.

It's death or slavery.

Faced with this impossible choice, The Babysitter howls anew. Tears are streaming down from beneath his mask. He falls on the floor and folds himself into a ball.

Papa sits down beside his defeated colossus, putting The Babysitter's head in his lap.

"There, there..." he pacifies, rubbing The Babysitter's back. It's a tender moment, the least he can offer after everything this enthusiastic recruit's already endured.

Papa takes a deep breath and begins to recollect. His voice becomes hypnotic.

"Did I ever tell you that Noodledome's the only one of those knuckleheads I truly trust?" he asks The Babysitter, who doesn't respond. "Pepe certainly has potential, but you can't bank on that. And trust me when I say, Mister Jumbo will be dead within a year at the rate he's going. As for Mister Blister, well... he may be getting too big for his bell bottoms. But not

Noodledome. Sweet, innocent Noodledome; he's my rock. Without him, I'm not even sure I'd want to be alive."

The Babysitter's beginning to settle. He knows, one way or another, it'll all be over soon. A hitherto unknown sense of tranquility washes over him.

"I've grown very fond of you too," Papa continues, affectionately rubbing The Babysitter's bald head. "Not as a confidant, of course. Not as a friend, no. As a human being, you're a despicable piece of shiftless shit, completely irredeemable. But as a hunter—you've become one of my favorites... Which is what makes this so difficult."

He cocks his gun and presses the barrel against The Babysitter's temple. He leans down and kisses his forehead.

"Oh, my boy," he laments softly. "Oh, my boy... you're an absolute... Doll!"

Papa Corn takes a deep breath. He uses this moment of temporary serenity to ponder the complexities and absurdities of life. The way random interactions can have such powerful consequences. And just when you think you've got everything figured out, something unexpected happens and shit goes sideways. Crazy.

Before he puts The Babysitter to sleep, he whispers,

"Papa loves you. Papa will always love you."

AFTERWORD

BILLY "BLOODY BILL" PON

Someone: *"Hey Billy, are you scared of clowns?"* Me: *"Actually, no. Not one bit. I'm only scared of diets and marriage."* That's one of two questions I get asked all the time. The second one is, *"Do you love clowns?"* To which I answer, *"No."* I know what you're thinking now: *"Why the hell would I make a horror movie about clowns then?"*

Well, that answer is easy. Because I felt like it was a challenge to not just *make* a clown movie but to make a *good* clown movie. 99.99999999% of clown horror movies are pretty tough to watch and cheesier than concession stand nachos. That's what inspired this film (with a little inspiration from the late great Sid Haig's performance as Capt. Spaulding in Rob

Zombie's *House of 1000 Corpses*). I have this belief that any movie can be a good movie no matter the genre.

Horror doesn't have to be the bastard red-headed stepchild that only produces silly movies with bad acting, writing, filming and special FX. I just want to entertain people and give them an escape from reality, if only for an hour and a half. So, *Circus of the Dead* was born there—alongside my local West Texas haunt "Circus of the Dead: Murder Maze" which ran 2004-2020. I used the haunt to build backstories, characters, scenarios and such with my childhood haunt designer and best friend Donzell Lee Ankrum.

One of those characters from the haunt was Doll Boy, played by my brother-in-law Serg Gracida. We figured before we do a feature film, we should get our feet wet with a short film, so we picked the chubby sledgehammer killer and *Doll Boy* became a reality. The short turned out really good, and that opened the door for us to tackle the feature film. Lee and I did our research when it came to studying real life circus clowns, as well as real life serial killers. All the clowns were based on us and our personalities. Yes, Papa Corn too. Papa, Corn (for us) was all the dark and bad about our inner subconscious that we would not (could not) ever show. We all innately have nasty thoughts. Papa has a nasty reality.

To say I'm surprised about the success of *Circus of the Dead* would be true. The film means so much to horror fans. They get the brutality of the film along with what I feel like is the most important thing if you want a good film: *heart*. That's what horror fans want. That's why *Texas Chainsaw Massacre* (1974) means so much to them. No matter how fucked up, horror-wise, a film is, it's gotta have that *heart* that moves the fan and takes them on a roller coaster ride in their minds while watching.

Entertain a horror fan and they will love you forever, and

the fact they love my film means more to me than any amount of money. There's lots of people making horror films these days but there's not a lot of good horror films being made. Filmmakers, take this advice from your old pal Bloody Bill: work harder! If you aren't good at a certain part of the filmmaking process, find someone to fill your weaknesses!

Have a good (honest) circle of people that are truthful to you and will tell you when you have a bad idea. Watch your film with no audio. Listen to just the audio of your film without the video. We are on this blue rock for a limited amount of time and there's only so many movies you can make. That movie will hopefully live longer than you... wouldn't you want to put your best foot forward and make some brilliant ass shit? A *classic* horror film can live forever! Inspire others, pay it forward, be humble, be hungry, be great!

Papa Corn the Clown was the best character I've ever written (so far)! Now we're on to ***Circus of the Dead 2*** and round two with Papa, Noodledome, Blister and Jumbo. My goal is to keep doing what we did right with the first film and fix what we feel we did badly. Will we succeed? You'll have to watch for yourself and get back to me!

Hugs & kisses....
Billy "Bloody Bill" Pon

ABOUT THE AUTHOR

Photo credit: Ama Lea

Over the past decade-plus, Joshua Millican has proven himself to be a horror expert of the highest caliber. After establishing a personal blog in 2011, Millican quickly became one of the horror genre's premiere journalists, contributing to many websites before ultimately landing at Dread Central in 2016. One of the top horror outlets on the planet, Millican served as Editor-in-Chief from 2019 through 2021. In addition to writing, Millican has been a member of numerous festival juries, a popular podcast guest, and has even scored a handful of acting gigs. His talk show *Chronic Horror* (sidelined by the Pandemic) explored the intersection of horror movie fandom and cannabis culture. Now married and a father for the first time, Millican pens hardcore horror/sci-fi/fantasy fiction like *Deeper Than Hell* and novelizations like *Forbidden Zone*.

Follow Joshua Millican on Twitter at @josh_millican.

Printed in the USA
CPSIA information can be obtained
at www.ICGtesting.com
CBHW011910291024
16595CB00012B/166